LITTLE, BROWN AND COMPANY
NEW YORK   BOSTON

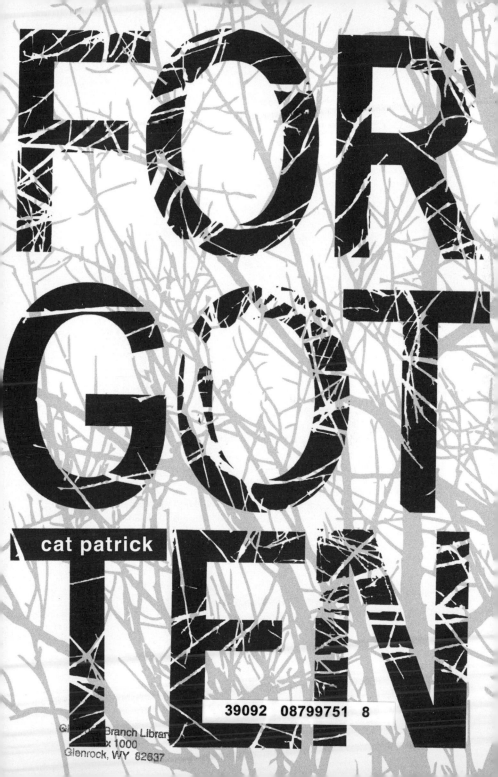

FOR
GOT
TEN

cat patrick

Little, Brown and Company

Hachette Book Group
237 Park Avenue, New York, NY 10017
Visit our website at www.lb-teens.com

Little, Brown and Company is a division of Hachette Book Group, Inc.
The Little, Brown name and logo are trademarks of Hachette Book Group, Inc.

The publisher is not responsible for websites (or their content) that are not owned by the publisher.

First Hardcover Edition: June 2011
First Paperback Edition: May 2012

Library of Congress Cataloging-in-Publication Data

Patrick, Cat.
  Forgotten: a novel / by Cat Patrick. — 1st ed.
      p. cm.
  Summary: Sixteen-year-old London Lane forgets everything each night and must use notes to struggle through the day, but she "remembers" future events and as her "flashforwards" become more disturbing she realizes she must learn more about the past or it just may destroy her future with her family and the wonderful boyfriend whose very presence helps.
  ISBN 978-0-316-09461-0 (hc) / ISBN 978-0-316-09460-3 (pb)
  [1. Memory—Fiction. 2. High schools—Fiction. 3. Schools—Fiction.
4. Dating (Social customs)—Fiction. 5. Family Life—Fiction.] I. Title.
  PZ7.P2746For 2012
  [Fic]—dc22
                                        2010043032

10 9 8 7 6 5 4 3 2 1

RRD-C

Printed in the United States of America

This is for my girls.
Later, when books are for reading, not eating,
I hope you'll be proud.

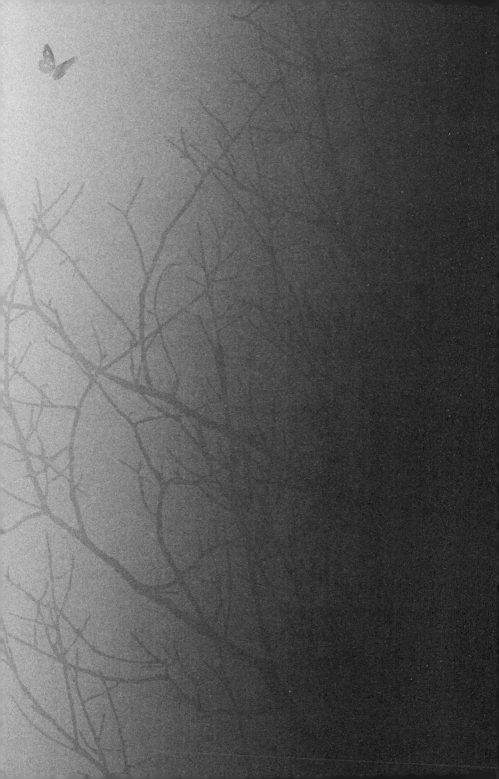

Nothing fixes a thing so intently in the memory
as the wish to forget it.

— Michel de Montaigne

Friday

10/14 (Thurs.)

Outfit:
—Straight-leg jeans
—Navy tunic with the little flowers (wasn't dirty—back in the closet)
—Blister-inducing red flats

School:
—Bring book for English
—Get Mom to sign permission slip for History

—Spanish quiz tomorrow (not on syllabus)
—Read over History homework in the morning...
too tired...

Notes:
—Ate tons of carbs today. (Mom bought mint chocolate chip ice cream!) EXERCISE!
—Ordered tights for Halloween

1

Aren't Fridays supposed to be good?

This one started badly.

The note on my nightstand didn't tell me anything useful. My eyelids wanted to stay closed; my favorite jeans were in the hamper; and there was no milk in the fridge.

Worst of all, my cell phone was dead: the shiny, candy red one that I'll have until it falls into a gutter; the one that has the calendar and reminder bells and is essentially my portable, socially acceptable security blanket.

"You'll be fine," my mom said during the drive to school this morning.

"How do you know?" I asked. "I could have a huge

math test today. There could be a school assembly that I won't know about."

"It's just one day, London. You'll be fine without your phone for one day."

"Easy for you to say," I muttered, looking out the window.

Now, right now, standing here, I have proof that my mom was wrong. I am not fine without my phone for one day.

Today is the day that I needed a new T-shirt for gym class. Had it not been dead, my phone, the phone my mom and I programmed together at the start of the year with important little reminders like this one, would have instructed me, in its tiny block lettering, to bring a shirt for Phys. Ed. today.

Therefore, today is the day I'm standing in gym shorts and my winter sweater, wondering what to do.

I can't very well wear a sweater for basketball (which is what we're playing, according to the board near the locker room door), so I ask Page if she has an extra top. We won't ever really be friends, but she still responds overenthusiastically. "Sure, London, here you go. Forgot your clean shirt again, huh?"

Again?

I make a mental note to jot myself a real note later, while at the same time wondering why today's note didn't mention bringing a gym shirt.

Page interrupts my train of thought. She smiles and hands me a bright yellow oversized tee with a beaming cat on it that reads: HAVE A PURR-FECT DAY!

"Thanks, Page," I grumble as I take the shirt from her and quickly put it on. It nearly covers the shorts—shorts!—that I'm already wearing. Why my locker contained shorts and not some other warmer, cuter piece of bottom-covering sportswear, I have no clue.

Note to self: add "bring pants" to note to self, too.

I feel like Page is watching me. I glance at her and, yep, she's watching me. We exchange pleasant nods before I throw my street clothes into the locker, slam it, and head out to the gym.

As I walk, two thoughts run through my mind. First, I wonder whether Ms. Martinez will let me go to the nurse's office for a Band-Aid to cover the painful heel blister that I can feel grating against my sneaker with every step. And, second, I can't help but thank my lucky stars that only the twelve other hapless souls with first-period gym class will see me in this hideous ensemble.

Unfortunately for me, Ms. Martinez is a coldhearted woman.

"No," she says, when I ask to go to the nurse's office before the game begins.

"No?" I ask in disbelief.

"No," she says again, black eyes daring me to argue. She holds her whistle at the ready.

I'm not stupid, so I don't press the issue. Instead, I hobble back to the bench, join my teammates, and vow to play through the pain.

Then halfway through what I can only assume is the lowest-scoring basketball game in high school sports history, a noise ricochets through the echoing gym that all at once makes my arm hairs stand on end, my eardrums seize up, and my teeth chatter.

For a moment, I don't know what's going on.

Ms. Martinez waves her arms in the direction of the exit, and my classmates begin lazily walking toward the doorway.

That's when I get it.

We are having a fire drill.

We, the students of Meridan High School, are going outside. All 956 of us. While I, London Lane, am sporting a bright yellow cat T-shirt that says HAVE A PURR-FECT DAY! and too-short shorts for the entire student body to enjoy.

Yep, it's a good Friday indeed.

2

The gymnasium is close to an exit, so we're among the first to make it to the safety of the faculty parking lot. Surrounded by the odd assortment of vehicles, from a station wagon here to a cherry red Porsche there, I watch apathetic students saunter out of the concrete block that is our high school, as if they're impervious to fire.

Not that I believe there's a fire.

My guess is that some moron pulled the alarm to be funny, not having the foresight to realize that he or she would then be forced to stand in the cold for an hour while waiting for the fire trucks to arrive and the firemen to clear the building and finally make the screeching alarm stop.

It's windy, and I think I see snow flurries. With every gust, I pull myself tighter into a ball to try to stay warm.

It's not working.

I yank my hair out of its messy knot at the nape of my neck, hoping it will act as a scarf. Immediately, the wind sets flight to my bright auburn locks, and I am both blinded and repeatedly face-whipped.

As the hordes of students gather, I hear whispers and chuckles, presumably about my outfit. I swear I hear the click of a camera phone, but by the time I peer through my wild mane, the photographer has hidden the evidence. Still, the trace of giggling from the inside of a tight circle of cheerleaders makes me nervous.

I stare at their backs until Alex Morgan whips her head of shiny black hair in my direction and locks eyes with me. She looks like she took time to apply an extra layer of jet-black eyeliner before evacuating the building.

Priorities.

Alex smirks at me and turns back to the huddle, and more giggles erupt from it.

At this moment, I wish for my best friend, Jamie. The girl has her faults, but she'll never back down from a cheerleader's slams.

Alone with my bare legs and purr-fect T-shirt, I hear bits and pieces of conversations about weekend plans, the "test we're missing right now," and "let's just take off and drive to Reggie's for breakfast, since we're already out here." I hug my arms to my torso even tighter, partially to shield myself from the weather and partially to obscure the cat.

"Nice T-shirt," says a smooth male voice, with just a touch of mockery. Using my left hand as a makeshift ponytail holder, I grab all the hair I can catch and turn in the direction of the voice.

And then time stops.

I see the smile first. There is an unmistakable sweetness peeking through the teasing. My armor begins to crumble before I've made my way up to the eyes; what's left of it melts away at the sight of them. Sparkling pale cornflower blue with darker flecks, surrounded by eyelashes any girl would envy.

Looking at me.

Right at me.

Even more than his mouth, his eyes are smiling.

If there was something near me — a piece of furniture, even a nonhostile person — I might reach out and physically steady myself because I feel off balance in his presence. In a good way.

Wow.

And then it's all gone. The shirt, the phone, basketball, Alex Morgan.

There's nothing but the boy before me.

He looks like he belongs in either Hollywood or heaven. I could stare at him all day.

"Thanks," I say after who knows how long. I force myself to blink. His face looks familiar somehow, but only in the way that I want it to.

Wait, do I remember him?

Please, oh please, oh please let me remember him.

I thumb through years and years of faces in the album in my brain. This face is nowhere to be found.

For a glimmer of a second, I'm sad about that fact. Then my optimistic side springs forth. I'm probably wrong. He has to be in there somewhere.

Where were we? Oh, the outfit...

"I'm starting a new trend," I joke.

I shift my body so that the wind blows my hair out of my eyes; I force myself to notice something other than his.

"I like your shoes," I add.

"Uh, thanks," he says awkwardly as he, too, looks down at his chocolate brown Converse All Stars. With not much left to say about shoes, he unzips and removes his tan hoodie.

Before I know what's happening, he's draping it around my shoulders and it's like I'm protected from the world, not just the elements. The fleece lining is warm from his body and smells faintly of soap and fabric softener and just... guy. A perfect kind of guy.

He's standing a little close to me for being a stranger, now in just his own T-shirt. It looks vintage; I've never heard of the band.

"Thanks," I say again, as if it's one of only ten words I know in the English language. "But aren't you cold?"

He laughs, as though that's the most ridiculous question in the world, and says, simply, "No."

Can't guys be cold?

"Okay. Well, thanks," I say, for the millionth time in two seconds.

What is it with me and that word?

"It's really no problem," he says. "I figured you could use it. You're turning blue," he adds, nodding toward my legs. "I'm Luke, by the way."

"London," is all I can manage.

"Cool name," he says with an easy smile. I can see a hint of a dimple in one of his cheeks. "Memorable," he adds. Very funny, I think.

A shriek pulls me from my Luke-induced trance.

"London, WHAT are you wearing?" Jamie Connor screams so loudly that at least five people stop their conversations and turn toward us. "Please tell me you have pants on."

I take back my wish for her to appear. She can go away now.

"Shhh, Jamie, people are staring," I say, pulling her close to me to try to shut her up. I can smell the perfume that my best friend will wear forever.

"Sorry," she says. "But you're kind of a disaster," she adds with a little laugh. I frown at her.

"Bad morning?" she asks, looping her arm through mine.

"Yep," I answer quietly, still very aware that Luke is nearby. "I forgot my gym shirt. Again."

Jamie gives me a sympathetic shoulder nudge before changing the subject. "I don't even want to ask who lent you that one. Have you seen Anthony out here?" she asks as she searches the crowd. But then her interest in Anthony comes to a screeching halt when she spots Luke. My Luke.

"Hey," she says to him.

"Hey," he says back. He refuses to look right at Jamie; I might like it a little.

"Who are you?" she asks, head cocked like a curious cat.

"Luke Henry," he says, finally focusing on her for a blink. "It's my first day." He looks away again and scans the crowd, as if he's grown tired of being where he is. I notice that he keeps his head low, like he doesn't want to attract attention.

Jamie is not used to boys looking away, and, frankly, with the short skirt and tight top she's wearing, I'm surprised by Luke's disinterest. She shifts her weight, pops a hip, and continues.

"What year are you?" Jamie asks.

"Junior," Luke answers.

"Cool. Us, too," she says. I think she might be finished with the questions, but no such luck. "So, why start on a Friday?"

Luke glances at Jamie, then his eyes find mine and there it is again.

He's back.

"I didn't have anything better to do today," he says matter-of-factly. "We were unpacked. Why not?"

"I see...and where did you come from?"

Make it stop!

"I just moved here from Boston."

"You don't have an accent," Jamie points out.

"I wasn't born there."

"Gotcha," Jamie says as she flips her blonde hair out of her eyes. It's one of her signature moves—one she'll do in college and beyond—and, best friend or not, my claws are out.

My posture has obviously stiffened, because Jamie pulls back a little from me to examine my face. She looks at Luke, then back at me again.

"Hmm," she grumbles, and I'm terrified that she is going to state the obvious, but instead, she continues the third degree. "Well, where were you before Boston—"

Jamie is interrupted by the sudden, quiet calm. Alarm under control, Principal Flowers grabs his bullhorn and herds us back inside in a tone that says he loathes every waking minute spent in our presence.

Jamie and I look at each other, then burst out laughing at the booming voice coming from tiny Principal Flowers. At least that's what I'm laughing about.

When we recover, I look back at Luke. Well, I *want* to look back at Luke.

But he's gone.

I pan the crowd furiously, but all that stands out in the sea of drab colors are bright red, white, and black cheerleading sweaters. Definitely not what I'm looking for. I feel myself beginning to panic, in that way you do when you lose something you really love, like a favorite watch or pen or pair of jeans.

We're moving now, Jamie and I, arm in arm. In fact, I'm pretty sure that's why I'm moving: because Jamie is pulling me forward.

Finally, I see it.

My insides do cartwheels when I spy Luke's T-shirt making its way toward the building. His head hangs low and he walks slowly but with purpose, conveying untouchable coolness. I am thrilled by the sight of him, but then disappointed.

How could he just walk away like that?

We had a moment, didn't we?

We had a moment, he lent me his hoodie, and he left. And now, he's walking back to class like nothing happened. Like he never met an interesting, albeit vertically challenged, redhead.

We had a moment, and now Luke Henry from Boston is over it, and I'm gripping my best friend's arm so tightly at the sight of his backside that said best friend gives me a look and twists her arm free.

All at once, my morning dips again, and I feel lower than I did when I discovered that my cell phone was dead.

Funny how possibility can lift you. Funny how reality can slam you down.

I watch Luke's back from twenty feet behind as he strides down the PE corridor, past the locker rooms and the Driver's Education and ROTC classrooms, and toward the commons. It's as if nothing happened. Nothing at all. And who knows? Maybe it didn't.

But as Luke Henry rounds the corner and slips out of view, there is one thing I know for sure. One thing that gives me a glimmer of a shard of a bit of hope that we'll see each other again.

I'm still wearing his sweatshirt.

"Good day today?" Mom asks when I jump into the Prius.

"It was okay," I say, turning on the radio.

"You seem to have survived without your cell phone. Anything interesting happen?" She drives us out of the school lot and turns toward home.

Shrugging, I say, "A new guy started today."

My mom glances in my direction, then faces forward. I can tell she's trying not to smile, but her efforts aren't working.

"A cute guy?" she asks. I can't help but smile, too.

"Yes."

"What's his name?"

"Luke."

"Did you talk to him?" she asks.

"A little. We had a fire drill and we ended up standing near each other. He's pretty cool."

My mom is quiet a moment, probably sensing that I'm about to put an end to the conversation. But then, nosy as she will always be, she can't resist one more question.

"Was he in your notes this morning?" she asks casually. I consider changing the subject or cranking up the radio even louder, but since she's one of two people I can talk to about my condition, I turn to face her in my seat and answer.

"That's what's weird!" I say.

"What do you mean?" she asks excitedly.

"Well, he wasn't in my notes this morning, but I had this whole conversation with him and everything," I say. "It was bizarre."

"Maybe you just forgot to mention him," Mom offers. We're turning into our development now. I shake my head.

"Maybe," I say, not wanting to discuss him anymore. In truth, I know there's no way I would forget to mention Luke Henry.

We're almost home when my mom's cell phone rings from the center compartment. "Sorry, honey, I've got to grab this."

"No problem," I say, happy to be left alone to daydream.

In the middle of the night, pen in hand, the hope seeps out of me. Luke's hoodie is in the laundry, but his face is almost gone. For three hours, I've tried to attach him to my forward memories. I've quizzed myself: Do we share a class? Will we go out? Will I know him for years to come? But with the clock counting down to 4:33 AM—the time when my mind resets and my memory is wiped clean—I have to admit that Luke Henry is nowhere to be found.

He's not in my memory, which means he's not in my future.

When I finally accept it, the truth stings. But there's no time to dwell on it, and there are only two choices: I can remind myself about someone who is not a part of my life, or I can leave him out of my notes to save myself from going through this all over again tomorrow.

This late, with my mind just minutes from "reset," it doesn't seem much of a choice at all. I grit my teeth and grip the pen and do what I have to do.

I lie to myself.

3

The house is still; it's early.

I check out the bedroom, trying to pinpoint differences between two nearly identical pictures: the one I remember from tomorrow and the scene before me now.

There's an empty mug with a used tea bag wound around the handle on a coaster on the desk. There's a sweatshirt hanging over the edge of the hamper like it's trying to get out. Tomorrow, the mug will be gone. There will be textbooks on the desk; the hamper will be empty.

I hold a note that explains what I've missed. Well, at least the highlights.

10/17 (Sun.)

Outfit:
　　—Supersoft boy's hoodie (Fri. note said I got it from the reject pile at school)
　　—Black leggings
　　—Sherpa boots

School:
　　—Bring Band-Aids for almost-healed blister
　　—Bring yoga pants, T-shirt for gym (had to borrow awful clothes from Page Fri.)
　　—CELL PHONE (Mom has it in the car)

Other stuff:
　　—J was in L.A. this weekend w/her dad
　　—Avoid Page this week
　　—Doctor this morning (tripped Fri. in PE)

I set aside the note and read through similar messages from the past week, paying particular attention to Friday's comments on clothes and school stuff. Then, still feeling like I'm walking into the world partially blind, I haul myself from bed and start the day.

On the way to the doctor's office, Mom takes Hudson Avenue, which cuts through the city cemetery. At the intersection of Hudson and Washington, we get caught at the light.

"We're going to be late," my mom mutters under her breath. She drums her hands on the wheel, and I wonder if she's missing a meeting to drive me.

I loll my head to the right side and scan the graves. They stand in formation, lines running straight away from me and then curving slightly in the distance.

The light turns green, and as the car speeds up, a movement catches my eye. Two people, a man and a boy, stop before a tombstone. In my rational brain, I know they're visiting a lost loved one. Nothing scary. But something about the mourners makes my shoulders tense and sends a shot of electricity through my body. I shiver in my seat; my mother doesn't notice.

"Do you remember what you're going to say when the doctor asks how this happened?" Mom asks, interrupting my thoughts.

"Yes," I reply, grateful for the distraction. "I tripped over a ball in gym class."

"Good," she says as we turn into the parking lot. She finds a space and we rush inside. We clear the lobby quickly and then ride the elevator up two floors in silence. All the while, my mind is still in the graveyard.

4

"Doctor's appointment?"

"Yep," I say, smiling my most innocent smile at Henne Fassbinder, school secretary and obvious lover of cats.

She frowns in response as she types something into my computer file with nails so long they'd have to open a soda can sideways.

I hop a little, hoping she'll hurry up. I want to get to my locker before class lets out—fewer opportunities for mistakes that way.

"In a hurry?" Henne asks.

"Nope," I say, trying another smile. She frowns again.

Finally, Ms. Fassbinder finishes typing and shoves back

in her swivel chair. She opens a cabinet and easily locates the file with my name on it and then inserts the note my mom wrote just minutes ago.

I assume that Ms. Fassbinder will wait until I'm gone to compare today's handwriting with that from previous days.

Turning around, I check the industrial clock mounted on the wall behind me. It's 9:52 AM. The bell will ring in three minutes, and I'm nervous about that, for some reason. I've missed PE, study hall, and Pre-calc. Not bad.

Finally, the secretary offers me a hall pass and I take it, but not before noticing the tiny decorative cats affixed to her nails. It looks like they were innocently walking through bright red cement when it set and trapped them forever.

Poor cats.

I hoist my bag onto my right shoulder and bolt from the office. I speed walk across the commons — ignoring the "badly bruised" ankle noted on my doctor's excuse — and start up the main hallway bordering the library. Halfway there, the end-of-third-period bell rings and I'm swimming upstream through distracted students, hand-holding couples, and ironclad cliques.

I try to avoid eye contact with everyone, but sometimes it's impossible. Page Thomas, looking like a D-list celebrity on her stylist's day off, approaches from the opposite direction and waves at me with what I consider to be a little too much enthusiasm. For a beat, I have no idea why she's so happy to see me. I shift my bag to my left arm so that I can cordially wave back as we pass.

Then I remember.

Soon she will corner me and ask me to set her up with Brad, from math. Ugh. Who am I, Cupid?

Where the main hall intersects with the pathways to the math and science wings, Carley Lynch and her circle have the hallway blocked. They're all in black and red uniforms, and a few squad members are actually taking notes as Carley speaks.

As I pass by, I notice a little Tigers mascot temporary tattoo high on Carley's perfect right cheekbone. I imagine her staring in her mirror this morning before school, trying to get the tattoo just so, which makes me giggle to myself.

Carley sees my expression and her eyes narrow. She makes a show of scrutinizing my outfit, then proclaims, "Hey, loser, props on getting yourself into a semidecent outfit today. Did you buy it at Kmart?"

Clueless as to where my clothes come from or why Carley hates me so much, I feel a lump rise in my throat. Even though I have the benefit of knowing that I'll grow more beautiful each day—and that Carley will never look better than she does right now—the comment stings. Just when I think I might lose it in front of the cheerleader cult, someone grabs my hand.

"Let's go," Jamie says softly before pulling me around the squad to my locker.

"I don't get it," I say quietly. Jamie shakes her head as she opens my locker door for me. I unload my book bag and take deep breaths in an effort to brush it off. While I do, Jamie leans against the locker next to mine, looking alarmingly like a hooker.

"Hey, Ma," Jason Rodriguez says to Jamie as he passes. "Nice legs."

"Thanks," she says back with a twinkle in her eyes.

I look at my friend, thinking that I both admire her and worry about her, despite knowing how things will turn out. Jamie is effortlessly surfer-girl pretty, even though she'll never hit the waves. Her chin-length dark blonde hair looks like she washed it in salt water and then let it dry in the warm sun, and her eyes are ocean green. She's stick-model thin, tanned, and sporting bare legs under a very short skirt with no tights. In October.

Down the hall, Jason high-fives his friend; I don't even want to know if it was about Jamie.

Jamie will always be *that* girl: the one boys love to flirt with—not date—and girls love to hate. And I will always be *that* girl's only friend.

"How did it go at the doctor?" Jamie asks. "I can't believe you fell again. You're such a klutz."

"Ha-ha," I say sarcastically. "The doctor was fine. He didn't ask much so I didn't have to lie."

"That's good."

"Yeah," I say, retrieving my Spanish book. "How's your day?"

"The worst!" Jamie begins as I slam my locker shut. "I got detention."

"What for?"

"We had a History test and I didn't study, so I gave Ryan Greene's paper a tiny peek, and all of a sudden, Mr. Burgess was standing over me. Anyway, detention starts at the ungodly hour of seven in the morning, and I have to go for like two weeks. Doesn't that seem a little unfair to you?"

Not waiting for me to respond, she continues. "I don't even know where detention is. I guess I better figure that out before seven tomorrow."

Jamie is quiet for a second, and then something pops into her brain.

"Hey!" she says, hitting me softly on the arm. "Why didn't you warn me about Mr. Burgess? About getting caught? You had to see that one coming."

"I guess I didn't," I say, shrugging. "It wasn't in my note this morning. Sorry."

"That's okay," Jamie says. "After tomorrow, I'll no longer be a detention virgin."

We laugh, but there's a pit in my stomach. This won't be the last time Jamie will see the inside of the detention hall. However, it will be the first time she'll flirt with the detention hall monitor, Mr. Rice, and the beginning of a sordid affair that will end in his divorce and Jamie's being sent to an all-girls' camp this summer to learn the difference between right and wrong, with the help of poetry, pottery, and Jesus.

I shake it off and Jamie rattles on while we move toward Spanish. We're nearly the same height today because I'm in high boots, but she walks taller, with confidence, and meets the eyes of passing students. I watch their shoes as they go by, imagining who might be wearing them.

White cross-trainers with laces and swoosh that exactly match the school's crimson?

Too easy.

Cheerleader.

Adidas tennis shoes with athletic socks?

Male soccer player in the off-season (noticed the hairy legs).

Are those bedroom slippers? Come on.

Ooh, here come some cute red boots. They're Western meets modern, and I want to borrow them. Who could it be? Maybe next year's homecoming queen, Lisa Something? She's trendy.

Unable to stand the suspense, I look up to find that I'm wrong. The girl in the boots is Hannah Wright. I can't help but smile, because Hannah's future is bright: in just a few years, she'll be a country superstar.

Too bad I can't tell her.

Back to my game, I see brown Converse All Stars coming toward me — actually head-on toward me — but before impact or identification, Jamie tugs me out of the way. We've made it to the Spanish corridor.

"Were you playing that stupid foot game again?" she asks, dropping my arm.

I shrug in response.

"Well, you should watch where you're going. You almost got run down by that weirdo," she says as we walk into Ms. Garcia's classroom.

"What weirdo?" I ask, intrigued. This morning's note mentioned nothing about a weirdo.

"That weird guy you were talking to during the fire drill. Jake. No, Jack. Lance? Whatever. You know, the guy who just moved here. He looked like he wanted to talk to you just now, but you were too busy looking at his feet. It doesn't matter, because you shouldn't be associating with weirdos. You're already weird enough as is."

Jamie turns and gives me a silly grin before the bell rings and ends our conversation.

When Ms. Garcia grabs a dry-erase marker and begins writing today's class agenda, I lean over and whisper gently to my best friend.

"Jamie, you look pretty today."

"Thanks, London," she says with a soft smile before turning in her seat toward Anthony Olsen, who is very openly eyeballing her legs.

5

It wasn't a dream: I wasn't asleep.

Almost, but not quite.

There, in that space between resting and REM, the image slammed into my head like a freight train. Now I'm sitting up straight, blinking furiously as if that will make my eyes adjust more quickly, breathing heavily, and sweating even though the heater's turned down low, as it will be every night for as long as I live here.

Like that gory photo in my Anatomy book that I'll encounter in a few months and can't stop thinking about already, the memory won't go away.

I want to walk down the hall and crawl into bed with my mom.

Instead, I try to self-soothe.

I take at least five deep, calming breaths, maybe more. I identify every dark shape in the room as nonthreatening. Finally, I burrow back inside the still-warm cocoon between two oversized pillows that form an upside-down V at the top of my bed.

Feeling a little better, I trick my brain into thinking about other things. The annoying doctor this morning; Jamie flirting with Jason; Jamie flirting with Anthony. White shoes, red boots, silly slippers, black shoes, brown sneakers...

Wham!

My eyes are open wide once more.

I try shaking my head. I try thinking of the shoes again. I even try thinking of other unpleasant thoughts, like Jamie's upcoming...situation.

Nothing works.

Exhaling loudly, I decide to let my mind go. Trying not to think about it is only making it worse.

I pull the blankets up to my chin and blink into the pitch-black bedroom.

And suddenly, I'm in a cemetery.

Being there makes me shiver now.

I'm at a funeral. At least I think I am.

I can't distinguish much except for hazy black shapes that could be people, and neutral stone beyond them in every direction. In my nostrils: the unmistakable scent of fresh-cut grass. It could be 8:30 AM or 3:14 PM. It's overcast: I can't tell.

I don't understand the scene, but it makes me feel heavy just the same.

And alone.

And afraid.

I consider whether to turn on the lamp and add details of this memory to today's note — right underneath musings about the "weirdo" that Jamie mentioned — but, ultimately, I stay where I am.

It's obvious that the mourners today triggered this particular memory. But knowing why doesn't soften the blow of the harsh underlying reality.

I remember forward.

I remember forward, and forget backward.

My memories, bad, boring, or good, haven't happened yet.

So, like it or not — and like it I don't — I will remember standing in the fresh-cut grass with the black-clad figures surrounded by stone until I do it for real. I will remember the funeral until it happens — until someone dies.

And after that, it will be forgotten.

6

I'm early to study hall.

I changed out of my gym clothes quickly in order to dodge Page Thomas's simple request, which is silly, because I remember when it'll happen...not today. But still, I rushed. I skipped the pointless trip to my locker near the math corridor and, voilà! Here I am.

Early.

This must be out of character for me, because Ms. Mason is eyeing me like I'm something disgusting she's been asked to ingest. I smile at her, and she looks away.

More students arrive. I take the Pre-calc. textbook and workbook from my bag, as well as a red mechanical pencil. Thankfully, none of the other students sit at my table, so I can spread out.

I begin the homework that this morning's note said I neglected to do last night. The other students are chatting among themselves, getting in those last bits of gossip before the bell rings.

"We meet again," says a smooth male voice out of nowhere.

I figure he's talking to someone at the next table, but I look up from my work anyway.

Then I suck in my breath.

The boy standing there across the table, looking like he's going to sit down with me, is flat-out gorgeous.

"Hi?" I say, more question than greeting.

"I didn't know you had study hall this period," the boy says, casually dropping his bag onto a chair and pulling out the one beside it. He sits down, his eyes never leaving mine.

Do I know him?

"Obviously," I say back, which comes out sounding a little snippy because I'm preoccupied.

Am I in the right place?

I scan the faces of my classmates. Andy Bernstein. Check. Hannah Wright. Check.

Tomorrow is Wednesday, so today is Tuesday. Check.

Second period?

Yep, I just had PE.

The boy is talking again.

"...because after the fire drill I had to finish orientation, and it took up all of second period, too. But you weren't here yesterday. Where were you?"

I'm tapping my pencil on my notebook now. This conversation is making me anxious. I think back to my notes before answering.

"At a doctor's appointment," I say, adding no additional clarification.

"Oh, sorry," the boy says, glancing down at the table for a moment. "I didn't mean to pry."

He looks embarrassed. It's cute.

"It's okay," I say, still tapping my pencil. "I tripped over a ball in gym. My mom thought my ankle was sprained."

"Was it?"

"Nope, just bruised," I say.

I'm tapping faster now.

He's still looking right at me.

Right into me.

Seriously, do I know him?

"That's good," he says. The bell rings and we're still staring at each other, him looking amused and me probably looking like I'm going to explode. At least that's how I feel.

"You okay?" he asks, with the slightest nod in the direction of my furiously tapping pencil. The acknowledgment of my nervous energy makes me fumble; I lose my grip, and the pencil launches into the air and then falls onto the floor. Feeling like a complete idiot, I scoot back in my chair and bend over to retrieve it. I grab the pencil, and, on my way back up, I spy something interesting.

Chocolate brown Converse All Stars.

My heart leaps as I remember this morning's note. This boy is my weirdo.

My weirdo is hot.

Somehow I manage to sit straight and scoot back to the table without completely humiliating myself. I smile at him. He smiles back, and I smile more.

"So, you stole my sweatshirt, you know," he says with a glint in his eye. "You can borrow it for a while, as long as you..."

"Shhh." Evil Eye Mason interrupts with a sharp whisper from her perch.

"...promise to..." Weirdo attempts to continue in a whisper before Ms. Mason smacks her palm on her desk.

"Mr. Henry!" she shouts. Weirdo's mouth slams shut, and he grudgingly looks her way. I'm happy to know at least part of his name.

"Sorry," he says.

"I should hope so. You're new, so I'll give you a pass this one time. But understand, son, there is no talking in my classroom. This is a time for studying. Quietly. This is not social hour."

A couple of the other girls giggle softly. Ms. Mason kills their giggles with a glance. She reminds me of a bird. A very mean bird.

"Sorry," the boy says again before pulling a pad and some charcoal pencils from his bag.

I'm happy for all the information I'm getting. His last name is Henry. He's new to school. And he's an artist.

Before going to work, the boy smiles at me once more. While I'm left gooey from the sentiment, he opens his drawing pad and flips through a few sketches in search of a blank page. I can't help but notice both that he's talented and that his subject of choice is . . . intriguing.

Ears?

As if he can hear my thoughts, Mr. Weirdo Henry brushes a stray wave from his eyes and glances at me one final time. He shrugs and smiles slyly, as if to say, "So what? I like ears."

I shrug and smile back. What I'm trying to say without words, and what I hope he understands, is, "Hey, we all have our things."

He's back to drawing before I can give it another thought, and I'm forced to continue my math homework in silence. But halfway through problem number 3, something dawns on me: the boy's sweatshirt in my room has to be the one Weirdo Henry is talking about. Apparently it's not from the reject pile, like my note said.

So apparently I lied.

At midnight, I boot up my laptop. I can type faster than I can scribble. Besides, the note by my bedside is already cluttered with hearts in the margins and flowery words about a boy I just met today.

10/19 (Tues.)

Horrible memory popped into my head as I was falling asleep tonight. Worst I can remember, really. Can't see much...just know I'm in a crowd of people wearing black. Their faces are muddy, and someone is dead. At first, I thought it might be Mom's funeral, but then I remembered hearing her sobs. She's there, too. Alive.

Can hear the occasional bird, and weeping. The weeping is terrible so I focus on the birds. I think it's morning, but it's gray so I'm not sure.

Terrifying statue of a saintly woman (maybe an angel?) one plot over to the left...carved of green stone and looking like she's watching us.

I finish typing and save the file on my computer desktop, naming it, appropriately, Dark Memory.

I print the page and then place the typed note under the handwritten one; hearts and flowers over the black-and-white account of dark days ahead.

I climb back into bed and turn off the lights for the second time tonight, thinking of the boy whose first name I don't know, feeling guilty for thinking of him when there are bigger things ahead.

Somehow, amid all the conflicting emotions, sleep grabs my hand and pulls me under.

And then everything unwritten is gone.

7

On the way to school, I consider telling my mom about the funeral memory, until I realize that it might scare her. Not everyone needs to know what's coming.

After she drops me off, I head straight for the library. It's an even-block day, so I have periods 2, 4, 6, and 8: I'll never be so happy to miss first-period PE. The warning bell hasn't sounded yet, but I want to arrive early and compose myself for the guy from my notes.

Mr. Henry.

I make my way toward the tables at the back of the library and retrieve a compact mirror from my bag. I use my sleeve to fix my eye makeup and then exchange the compact for my Spanish book.

I don't hear him approach. Then, without warning, he's across from me, leaning on the table, eyes fixed on my face.

"Hey."

I lower the book and my jaw drops. I thought I was prepared, but no. Not for this.

"Hi," I manage.

"Good day so far?" he asks.

"Not really," I answer truthfully.

Concern crosses his face, and it warms me. "What happened?" he asks.

"Oh, nothing," I answer. "Just overslept and my mom was annoying and . . . nothing. Not worth talking about."

The bell rings, and he and I are eye-locked. When the shrill tone stops, he whispers, "Okay, but if you decide you do want to talk, you can tell me."

"Thank you," I say, meaning it.

"You're welcome," he says back in an intimate whisper, before he's hushed by Ms. Mason.

"Luke Henry and London Lane, this is your final warning. No talking!"

Warmth washes over me at the sound of his name next to mine, and as he searches through his crowded bag for schoolwork, I breathe his name so softly that I can barely hear it myself.

"Luke."

We can't speak the rest of the ninety-minute period, but his presence makes me feel better. It allows me to forget the frenzied morning and, more important, this morning's note.

Halfway through the period, my fingers accidentally brush Luke's across the table. It feels like someone shot adrenaline directly into my heart; I inhale sharply and quickly move my hand to my lap. Luke glances up at me and smiles, which makes me blush and look away. I hear him chuckle a little under his breath and then turn a page.

Aware that I can't seem to remember Luke from tomorrow or the future, all I want to do right now is ditch class and spend the rest of the day getting to know him before he disappears again. Instead, I sit, grabbing glimpses of him every so often, and try my best to act normal.

I answer the phone before my mom hears the ringtone and scolds me for being up so late.

"What's up?" I whisper.

"Were you asleep?" Jamie asks, more surprised than concerned that she might have woken me.

"No, but my mom thinks I am."

"Didn't you know I was going to call?" she asks.

"You know I don't remember today, only tomorrow on," I say, rolling my eyes at her, even though she can't see it.

"I know, I'm just kidding."

"Oh," I say, tired. "What's up?"

"I need to borrow that supercute green shirt you bought that time your mom took us to the city for your birthday."

I am silent. Of course I have no idea what trip she's talking about from the past, but I think forward to what she'll wear tomorrow.

"Hello?" Jamie asks.

"Sorry, I'm here; sure, it's fine," I say in a low tone. "You're coming over before school to get it, right?"

"Yes, but remember I have detention, so it's going to be..."

"Shhh!" I interrupt. The floorboards are creaking outside my room. "My mom's coming. Gotta go!"

I hang up and toss the phone on the nightstand just as my mom peeks into the room.

"Honey, it's late," she says.

"I know, I was just going to sleep."

Mom gives me a look.

"What?" I ask.

"Are you sure you weren't talking on the phone?" She smiles in that way that tells me I've been caught. And yet, for no particular reason, I deny it.

"I'm sure," I say, inching under the covers. "Will you turn off the light?" I ask. She does.

"Night, Mom," I say, yawning for effect but meaning it, too.

"Good night, London," she says, and before I hear her own bedroom door click shut, I'm asleep.

8

I'm shivering in my closet, wearing only a bra, tank top, and underwear, wet hair dripping down my back, when Jamie scares the crap out of me by appearing in the doorway.

"Morning," she says, with no warning whatsoever.

"What the hell!" I shout, jumping farther into the closet.

"Uptight much?" Jamie teases, taking in the clothes hanging neatly on the racks. "Wear this one," she says, pointing to a plaid miniskirt.

"That's way too short," I protest. "I have no idea why I own that."

"I made you buy it," she says proudly. "I love that skirt."

"You can have it," I say, turning away from her and continuing my clothes fit. "What are you doing here so early?" I ask casually.

"You are so mental," Jamie says. "We talked last night. I'm borrowing..." She moves to a row of shirts and quickly looks through them. She locates the sleeve she seeks and yanks the item off the hanger. "... this green shirt today."

"Cute," I say.

"I know," Jamie agrees. She drops her bag and coat to the floor, swaps her own shirt for the green one, then puts herself back together, leaving her shirt in a heap on my closet floor.

"Don't you want this?" I ask, picking it up.

Jamie shrugs. "I'll get it later. See you in Spanish."

And with that, she is gone.

"Leaving already?" Page Thomas asks anxiously as I slam my PE locker shut. "Man, you're fast."

"Yeah, I need to get going," I say over my shoulder to her. "See you tomorrow."

"Monday," Page corrects me, her voice raining disappointment.

"Oh, right, Monday," I reply loudly, now all the way to the heavy locker room doors. Page is following me.

"Wait, London?" she asks. "Can I talk to you for a minute?" I sigh, knowing what's coming.

"Sure," I say, with as much enthusiasm as I can muster

through my utter disappointment. I want to leave and go meet him.

"Thanks," Page says, beaming. I notice that her icy blue eyes are so light they nearly match the whites. With those and her almost silvery blonde hair, she looks like an ice princess.

An ice princess who wears outdated glasses and baggy, mismatched clothes that could one day land her on a makeover show.

I stare at Page until she speaks.

"Okay, so I feel a little silly asking you this," she begins, "but that day when I was on office duty and delivered that note from your mom to your math class, I noticed that Brad Thomas sits next to you and I was wondering if you know if he has a girlfriend?"

Brad Thomas. I'll sit next to him in math for the rest of the year. His handwriting looks like a third grader's; I know from sneaking a peek at his test to see his score in a couple weeks. Beyond that, he's definitely not a math genius, either.

Stalling, I look around to see if anyone's watching us. My eyes land on Page's backpack: her name is embroidered there. Page Thomas.

"You like a guy with the same last name as you?" I ask randomly.

"Yep," Page admits freely, like she planned it that way. "Convenient."

More like gross.

Now Page is the one staring. Expectantly. I know I need to say something, but I'm not sure what. I can't tell her that I remember what happens to her—that Brad will break her heart—but I need to go. The clock is ticking, and, beyond the fact that I desperately want to meet Luke Henry, I also can't be late to class. Detention with Jamie and her train wreck is not something I want to witness firsthand.

"Page, I have to go. I'm going to be late," I say. Her smile slides off her face, but she doesn't speak.

"Listen, I don't really know Brad," I continue. "We're not friends or anything, so I don't have a clue if he's dating anyone. I'm sorry."

Her face is so low it might actually touch the ground. Apparently I'm her only hope, which is ironic, if you think about it. The person who can see the end is the one she's counting on at the beginning.

All I want to do is leave, but I feel trapped by Page's pleading eyes. With no apparent way out, I consider what she's asking. Would she get over Brad if I told her he was going to humiliate her and break her heart? Probably not. She'd call me crazy and find another way to date him.

That thought in mind, I surrender.

"All right, I'll try to strike up a conversation with him and get some information. Soon, okay?"

Page beams and hugs me with a squeal, then takes off. I follow her into the commons, then turn right when she goes straight. I race up the hallway that leads to the library, making a mental note as I go to include the promise in my end-of-the-day recap. I also make a mental note not to obsess about the wrongness of moving this forward.

Page may not know for sure what's coming like I do, but every relationship has the potential to fail. Somewhere deep inside, she has to know that's a possibility. And yet, she's okay with it. That's enough for me.

I try not to think of my own warning sign with Luke—the big flashing one that says YOU DON'T REMEMBER HIM!—but I ignore it for the possibility of a relationship. I guess that makes me a little like Page.

A boy I don't recognize accidentally bumps me as he rushes by. He is decent-looking, and I can't help but wonder: Was that Luke? I watch some of the other male faces blow past, all at once struck by the realization that I don't have a clue what Luke looks like. He could be walking next to me right now and I wouldn't know it. What if he thinks I'm a freak for not talking to him? What if he doesn't like how I look?

I take cover in the girls' bathroom to get my anxiety in check. Then, I scan myself in the mirror for anything that might turn Luke off. Thankfully, I'm completely alone as I fix a weird piece of hair and check my teeth, nose, and butt in the mirror.

The bell rings as I leave the bathroom; I run the rest of the way to the library.

"Tardiness is unacceptable," Ms. Mason says to me without looking up from her magazine. I move toward the only open seat: the one across from a boy who looks very happy to see me.

Somehow I know: this is Luke.

As I sit down, he casually slides a piece of notebook paper across the table, then returns to whatever he was working on. I unpack my schoolwork before reading the page; the wait is excruciating, but I don't want to seem too eager. When I do read what he's written, I fight hard to keep my expression in check.

London,
    It seems we have a problem chatting in class. How about you give me your number and we can try it later?
                                        Luke
PS—You look nice today.

I press my cheek to my shoulder to stifle a snort. Luke wrote the note before I got here; he had no idea how I looked before I sat down.

For the remainder of the period, I daydream about a future with Luke like normal girls who can't remember the future might do with a crush. At least that's the bright side of forgetting him each night: I can wonder.

Two minutes before the bell, I scrawl my number on the bottom of Luke's note and pass it back. I am surprised when he risks detention by pulling out his cell phone and saving my number right then and there. Thankfully, Ms. Mason doesn't notice.

When the bell rings, Luke and I stand at the same time and walk together to the library doors, close but not touching. Hannah Wright leaves before us and holds the door so it doesn't slam in our faces. She looks from me to Luke to me again, then smiles encouragingly before turning around. In the hallway, Luke and I turn to go in different directions.

"Talk to you soon," he says.

"Sounds good," I reply. I want to say more, but we are bottlenecking the main hallway, and there is only so much time between classes. Instead, I wave and turn away, forcing myself to walk, not skip, to my locker.

Later, in World History, Mr. Ellis says he's going to show a film about Nazi Germany.

"It's disturbing, but I expect you all to act like mature adults. Anyone who cannot do that will be sent to the office."

After study hall with Luke, I'm still feeling more like a giddy schoolgirl than a mature adult. I try to muzzle my permagrin, but it can't be contained. I turn my head toward the window so Mr. Ellis doesn't see me smiling and take it the wrong way.

I'm surprised to discover huge white flakes of snow drifting lazily from the sky. The snow blankets the courtyard like froth on the top of a perfect latte. It's beautiful and untouched, and it calms me.

Giddiness now in check, I look back at Mr. Ellis, who is consulting a notebook on top of his desk. With his pointer finger as a guide, he scans a list. Then he looks up at me.

"London Lane, did you bring your permission slip today?" Everyone in the class turns to look at me. I can't help but flush because of the attention. For the moment, my grin is gone.

"Oh, sorry," I say, leaning over to snatch my bag from under my seat. Unless I put it there yesterday and forgot to remind myself, I know the permission slip isn't inside. Yet I make a show of looking for it.

"Sorry," I say after a few seconds. "I guess I forgot it again."

"Then you'll have to go to the library," says Mr. Ellis.

"Okay," I say, standing up, bag in hand. My face burns as I walk to the front to take the hall pass from Mr. Ellis's outstretched hand. I leave the classroom, and in the hallway my embarrassment quickly subsides. For forever, this is the type of slipup that I will loathe: the little mistakes that make me seem spastic.

But not today.

Today there is snow on the courtyard.

Today there is Luke.

9

Despite falling flakes obstructing my vision, I see Jamie's silhouette in the front window as I trudge around the corner to her street.

"Why aren't you wearing that cute coat you bought when we went thrifting?" she asks, even before the front door to her 1970s house is all the way open. "And why are you dressed like you're exploring the Arctic?"

"Why were you watching for me?" I answer her questions with a question as I kick snow off my boots and push past her into the entryway. I start to unravel.

"It's dark," she shrugs. Jamie will never admit it, but toward me, at least, she's very protective.

"Why did you walk here, anyway?"

"I don't know," I say, tossing wet hair out of my face. "Seemed like a good idea."

I finish unwrapping and then neatly stack my winter wear on the entryway bench. But not without grabbing my cell phone in case Luke calls tonight.

Just as we're ready to head to Jamie's room, her mother pops her head around the corner and beams at me. She's wearing a retro print apron over her power suit.

"Hi, London!" she calls.

"Hi, Susan," I say with a friendly wave. Jamie rolls her eyes, grabs my hand, and pulls me in the direction of the stairs.

"How are you, sweetheart?" Susan asks as we pass.

"I'm fine, thanks for asking," I call as I'm dragged down to Jamie's lair in the finished basement.

Halfway down the stairs, my mom calls to make sure I made it safely. I quickly tell her I'm fine and hang up.

Thirty minutes later, I'm on Jamie's bed, trying not to get bloodred nail polish on her comforter.

"Why do you have that weird look on your face?" Jamie asks. "You're making me nervous."

"I don't know," I say. "I'm just happy."

"About the weirdo?" Jamie teases.

"He's not weird; he's hot," I say back.

Jamie shrugs.

"So, what's the deal? Do you remember having babies with him or something?"

I set down my polish and look at my best friend intently.

"No," I say in a whisper. Jamie scoots closer to me. "I can't remember him at all."

"Then what's the point?" she asks, rolling her eyes and looking disappointed. She refocuses on her nails. "Why bother?"

"Well, that's the thing," I say. "If you think about it, it's not that he isn't in my future."

That gets her attention. She looks up. "Huh?"

"Well, I reread my notes from this week. Monday, I didn't remember Luke from Tuesday. But then on Tuesday, I talked to him and stuff. See?"

"Uh...no."

"He was in my future on Monday, I just didn't remember it. It's not that he isn't in my future...."

"Then it's probably because he'll do something bad to you. You're blocking him." Jamie sets down her nail polish and looks at me seriously. "London, you should stay away from that guy."

"It doesn't necessarily mean something that bad," I say, wanting to defend Luke. "I mean, he's not going to kill me or anything."

"How do you know?" Jamie asks.

"I just know!" I say, not really just knowing. But logically, I remember way into the future, so I assume that I won't be murdered anytime soon.

"Okay, okay!" Jamie playfully shouts, holding up her

palms in surrender. "I just think maybe you should aim a little higher."

I don't answer, for fear of what's coming next. I brace myself for the conversation that my note this morning told me we'd have here tonight.

"Take Ted, for example," Jamie begins. She means her detention monitor, who also happens to be the Driver's Education teacher. Who also happens to be married.

"What about him?" I groan.

"Hey, that's not nice," Jamie says with a babyish frown.

"He's married, Jamie," I say without looking at her.

I try to avoid remembering holding Jamie's hand at the side of her hospital bed after a bottle of pills doesn't work, but trying not to think of the memory only makes it burrow itself into my brain.

"He's unhappily married, and he's a really great guy." Jamie defends Mr. Rice as I defended Luke. I can't help but think of her own unhappy marriage to come, of stories of her parents' unhappy marriage that may have influenced her in some way.

It reminds me of a note I read this morning from last week.

"Hey, how's your dad?" I ask casually. Jamie and I will spend a college spring break at his house in L.A. "Didn't you visit him recently?"

She gives me a funny look. "Why are you acting like you know him? You've never even met him."

"Oh, sorry," I say. "Anyway, how was the trip?"

Jamie eyes me skeptically and applies some polish. "We already talked about this. The trip was fine. He's fine. His lame new wife is still lame."

"I wonder if my dad has a lame new wife," I say under my breath.

I tighten the cap on the potent red polish. "Do you have any black? My nails are chipped," I say, surveying the damage.

"Red on the bottom and black on the top, huh? Very school-spirited of you," Jamie comments as she digs through a basket of tiny glass bottles in every color. She finds black and tosses it my way. Still, she's focused.

"What's with the dad talk all of a sudden?" Jamie asks, but doesn't let me answer. "They're gone. End of story. Anyway, stop trying to change the subject. I'm serious about Ted. He's really great."

"Uh-huh," I murmur as I paint.

"He asked me to meet him after school on Monday," she says, as if it's the most natural thing on earth. I stop painting midnail.

"Jamie, seriously, you can't do that."

"Why not?"

She laughs like it's a game. She can't see what this fling will do to her down the line, but I can.

"Why not? I'll tell you why not."

"Go ahead, I'm listening," she says, but she picks up a bottle of hot-pink polish and goes to work on her toes.

"He's a teacher; you're a student. He's an adult; you're

a minor. It's illegal, Jamie. He could get fired and sent to jail."

"He won't. That never happens."

That never happens? Do we live in a world where this is so common that Jamie has grounds to say "that never happens"?

I ignore her and go on.

"He's old."

"He's only twenty-four," Jamie answers. "And have you *not* seen him? He's totally hot."

I think of passing Mr. Rice in the hallway next week: she's right, he is hot. But that doesn't make this okay.

I mentally consult my notes and recall the couple of mentions of guys Jamie has associated with recently. "Don't you like Jason? Or Anthony?"

"They're boys. They're fine distractions, but Ted is a man."

"He clearly has issues if he's pursuing a high school girl."

"I'm not just any high school girl. And really, London, you can't change my mind. I *like* him! Why can't you just be happy for me?"

My argument is going nowhere, so I bring out the big guns.

"Do I have to tell you how this will end?" I ask softly.

Jamie's head whips in my direction. She meets my eyes. In hers, I see a fire blazing.

"You won't tell me that I'm going to get caught cheating, but you'll happily wreck things with Ted?"

"Not happily, it's just that I . . ."

"Stop," she says, holding up a palm. "I don't want to hear it. We'll just sec. Okay? We'll see how things turn out. You could be wrong."

"I'm not," I say confidently.

"Whatever," Jamie snaps.

We are silent for a few moments. I consider the long walk home in the snow, and eventually I take one for the team.

"Sorry, J, I just worry about you."

"I know you do," she says. "But stop. I'm okay."

"I know you are," I say.

"Seriously, London, listen to me," Jamie begins, sitting up taller on the bed. "You can mess with your own business however you want, but keep those memories about me to yourself. It's weird enough knowing that you know how things will go for me. I'm not one of those people who go to palm readers. I like surprises. Just let me live my life." Before I can open my mouth, she adds, "Please?"

"I will," I promise sadly.

"Thanks," Jamie says with a weak smile.

I think we're okay now, but as we walk out of her bedroom to head upstairs for a spaghetti dinner, Jamie mutters, "You better write that down in your little notebook so you don't forget it."

"Don't worry," I say softly. "I will."

10

I'm in the cemetery.

My mother is sobbing to my right. There is a menacing stone angel to my left. Across a semicircle of black-clad mourners, a few faces stand out: an older woman with a white lace handkerchief, a younger woman in a low-cut dress, an imposing bald man who looks like a brick wall.

My eyes are stuck for a moment on a small black brooch attached to the older woman's sweater. From where I stand, it looks like a jeweled beetle, and it seems oddly fancy for a funeral. Then again, I vaguely remember reading an article later in life about Egyptians being buried with beetles. Maybe it's significant to her. Maybe she just likes bugs.

Tentatively, I inhale, fearing the stench of rotting corpses, but instead I smell two of my favorite scents: grass and rain. Some of the mourners have umbrellas. Some are getting wet.

I look at the path leading to our gathering: it is dirt and rock, mostly dirt in some places. Because of the rain, there are footprints there. Some small; some large. Lots of footprints.

I want to walk through the footprints and mess them up, but I don't. Instead, I stand still in the rain, wondering what's going on.

11

Eyes adjusted to the October morning, I try to read the note in the dark. No go.

I roll to my side and edge out from under the cozy comforter. Reaching to turn on the bedside lamp that I'll have for years to come, I knock over a cup of water that I don't remember leaving on the nightstand.

Rookie mistake.

Quickly, I snap on the lamp and mop up the small puddle with my pajama sleeve. The PJs are red thermal; I don't remember putting them on.

Situation under control, I sink back against the pillows. Squinting from the light, holding the note inches from my nose, I read.

10/24 (Sun.)

Clothes:
—Red thermal pajamas most of the day
—Long-sleeved teal sweater and skinny jeans
(Mom and I had dinner at Casa de Amigos...spilled
hot sauce on upper thigh of jeans...check to see if
stain's out)

School:
—Take Span.-Eng. dictionary to Spanish for
translation exercise
—Anatomy quiz (check out study guide by the
computer before school)
—Start on graphic design project

Other:
—J was still weird today about Friday's
conversation (told me again NOT to tell her anything
about her future)
—Notes about J & me talking about dads made
me curious...snooped in Mom's room today while she was
out. Insane what I found. Envelope in my right desk
drawer. Not sure what to do except keep it hidden from
Mom for now.
—Luke didn't call again today (read back; he
sounds awesome minus the no-calling thing)

I fling off the heavy quilt and plod over to the desk. I
grab the study guide from the top and the overstuffed

envelope from the drawer. On my way back to bed, my eyes wander to the framed photos of me and Jamie dating back to what looks like junior high. There is a silly collage with photos and magazine cutouts that I can only guess Jamie and I made together. It's juvenile, but I like it. Without being able to remember for sure, I assume that things were a whole lot simpler then.

Half an hour later, my mom knocks and I rush to cover up the pile of contraband. When I don't answer, she opens the door anyway.

"I knocked," she says.

"I know."

She looks at me quizzically in response to what I can only assume is an expression that is equal parts anger and guilt.

"You're going to be late for school," she says.

"Okay, I'll hurry," I say back.

"What's up?" she asks, a funny expression still plastered on her face.

You tell me, I think to myself.

"Nothing, why?" I say instead.

"You seem . . . off. You seemed off last night, too," she says, one hand on the open door and the other on the frame.

"Well, I'm not," I retort. She holds up her hands in surrender.

"Okay, fine, London. Just get moving. You're going to be late." She turns and closes the door behind her.

Twenty minutes later, during the ride to school, she interrupts my thoughts.

"Is this because of that boy?"

I whip my head in her direction. "Did you read my notes? That's a total invasion of privacy," I snap.

"Whoa," Mom says calmly. "I most certainly did not read your notes, London Lane. I would never do that. Why would you suggest such a thing?"

"Because you know about the guy."

"London, you *told* me about him," Mom says, with an annoying smile.

"Oh," I say, embarrassed. "Well, I don't want to talk about him."

"Whatever you say," my mom says, with a little laugh that makes me want to scream. Thankfully, we've arrived at the school.

The moment the car stops in the drop-off zone, I jump out, slam the door, and walk purposefully inside Meridan High.

As the morning progresses, my hostility toward my mother morphs into anger toward the world. When Jason Samuels accidentally hits me in the shoulder with the basketball during PE, I chuck it right back at him.

Hard.

When Page Thomas dares approach me about her stupid crush, I silence her with one knifelike look.

When the gorgeous Goth girl who will spend most

days in the parking lot for the rest of the year runs into me in the hallway, I don't apologize.

And when I throw open the library doors, storm through the metal detectors, and march to my seat for study hall, I'm ready to confront Luke about not calling or just ignore him completely.

But then he arrives. And speaks.

"Want to come to my house for lunch today?" he asks, all dimple and blue eyes.

"Yes," I say. "Yes, I do."

"What's that?"

Jamie is way too nosy. I've only opened my bag to put my Spanish textbook in it before class, and she's managed to log its contents in under two seconds.

"Nothing," I say, glancing at the manila envelope before zipping the bag and easing it onto my shoulder.

Jamie is staring at me. She's not buying "nothing."

"Fine," I say, pulling her away from my locker and in the direction of Spanish. "I'll tell you, but it's no big deal."

"Sounds interesting," she says, looping her arm through mine. Jamie and I will always walk like this: arm in arm. It's our thing and I like it, particularly this morning, when I'm feeling like I need her strength to get through what's ahead.

Then again, remembering this morning's note, I know that she needs my strength today, too.

Jamie is looking at me expectantly.

"It's some old photos and stuff," I say quietly, as if it's a secret.

"Of who?" Jamie asks.

"Of my dad," I say, wincing.

"You and the dad thing lately..." Jamie's voice trails off and she looks ahead to navigate us through the bustling hallway.

"I found them hidden in a box in my mom's closet with some of my dad's old ties and stuff."

"You were snooping around in your mom's closet?" Jamie asks, totally missing the point.

"Yes," I say without explaining. "Anyway, that's not the worst part."

"What's the worst part?" Jamie's pretty eyes are back on me now.

"He sent me some birthday cards when I was little," I say, feeling sick. Exactly three. Exactly three birthday cards that, apparently, my mother hid from me.

"What did they say?" Jamie asks, intrigued.

"Just normal stuff," I lie. In truth, the cards are depressing. They're sparse and apologetic.

But they're there.

Jamie and I walk in silence the rest of the way to Spanish, me thinking about my dad, Jamie gripping my arm tightly because I think she knows she needs to right now.

12

"Is that him?" Jamie whispers as she leans forward toward me. Our desks are pushed together, head to head. We're supposed to be translating a Spanish newspaper article into English.

Instead, Jamie is flirting with Anthony and I am looking at faded photographs that I've expertly hidden within the pages of my Spanish dictionary.

"I guess so," I whisper back.

I'm not sure why we're whispering: we're supposed to talk during language lab. Ms. Garcia looks at us funny, so Jamie translates the headline of the story.

EARTHQUAKE SHAKES MEXICO CITY

"*El terremoto...*" She reads aloud in Spanish as she writes the phrase, accentuating the tongue roll to make me giggle. I know she's trying to lighten the mood.

I hear Amber Valentine behind me, struggling to pronounce "*hambre*," or *hungry*. Giving up, she decides to amuse her partner by saying "*tengo hamburger*," and I suspect the reason he laughs so hard at her stupid joke is that Amber Valentine looks like someone named Amber Valentine.

"Let me see another one," Jamie commands when she's finished writing. I offer her the dictionary with the photos inside.

As she checks them out, I look at the pictures upside down and backward, thinking to myself that my dad looks exactly as I'd imagine him to look.

He has kind eyes and a huge, openmouthed grin. Clearly, I got my hair color from him, but his skin is ghost-like and freckled, whereas mine is more creamy porcelain, like Mom's. Wearing 90 SPF sunblock, I am capable of getting a tiny tint of tan; I see from photos that Dad is either white or burned.

I can almost hear an easy, booming laugh erupting from the worn images. His uniform of choice seems to be faded jeans and untucked shirts, and in it, he's big and strong, ready to fight off monsters real or imagined.

Jamie pauses at a photo of my father teaching a preschool-aged me to swim. In the picture, he's looking at my younger, more scraggly self with a mixture of admiration, curiosity, and blatant love. I feel like I'm going to cry.

Jamie glances my way and then turns the page.

"Is this your grandmother?" she asks quietly.

"Where?" I say, leaning toward her now. She turns the book in my direction and points to the background of a photo of my dad holding baby me.

There, standing behind us, is someone I hadn't even noticed.

Someone I don't know, but recognize.

Someone I haven't met yet, but will.

My heartbeat quickens as I grab the dictionary and yank it back to my side of the desk island. I lean in closer and closer still, wishing that I had one of those tiny magnifying glass things that diamond dealers use.

There, in the middle of Spanish, with Jamie staring at me like she's embarrassed to know me, something clicks.

The woman in the background of the photo is very clearly my grandmother. She is looking at baby me with such love and devotion that it almost hurts.

More than her expression, her appearance is the dead giveaway. Her hair matches mine and my father's, and much of the rest of her is carbon copied in him and sprinkled in me.

"Twenty minutes," Ms. Garcia calls to the class, interrupting my analysis.

Jamie mutters something profane under her breath and grabs our paper. She begins furiously translating.

"Want help?" I offer.

"No, keep obsessing," she says without looking up.

"Thanks."

"No problem."

Twenty minutes later, Jamie has turned in the lab paper we'll get back next week with a bright red B+ on top, and we're gathering our things. I'm carefully sliding the dictionary back into my bag, trying not to let any photos loose.

"What are we doing for lunch?" Jamie asks, slinging her bag over her shoulder. Just then, I remember what I'm doing. I straighten up and look at my friend.

"Luke asked me to lunch today," I say.

"Oh," she says, sounding disappointed. I think I see a flash of something in her eyes. Annoyance? Jealousy? "That's okay, I'll go with Anthony."

"Sorry, J."

I notice then that Anthony is leaving in a hurry, and I wonder how she'll really spend her lunch hour.

As I walk to meet Luke, my mind is on the photos. One photo, really. One person, specifically: my grandmother.

I can't believe that I didn't recognize her this morning. Now, I consider what that recognition means.

On one hand, I have an older, wiser role model who (presumably) loves me and might want to bake me cookies and braid my hair. Well, okay, just the cookies.

But on the other hand, my single future memory of her is the darkest one I've got: my grandmother is the older woman wearing the pretty beetle brooch at the funeral.

My brain twists and turns as I round the corner to the

commons. I see Luke leaning against the far wall, bag dropped to the floor next to him. His eyes are cast down; he appears to be deep in thought. As soon as I wonder what he's thinking about, his eyes are on mine. He smiles, pushes off the brick wall, and picks up his bag.

For some reason, my brain chooses that exact moment to figure it out. I stop halfway across the commons. A boy nearly collides with me. Luke looks confused.

The funeral.

Grandma.

Mom.

There is only one logical explanation. I don't want to think it but the thought shoves its way to the front of the line anyway.

It's Dad's funeral.

My dad is going to die.

There.

Thought.

13

I am almost completely distracted by Luke by the time we make it through rows of student cars and reach his...

Minivan?

He laughs at my baffled expression at the sight of a car usually reserved for soccer moms. Apparently it was his soccer mom's car before she replaced it with an oh-so-economical SUV.

As he starts the engine, Luke confirms that, yes, I'm still fine with going to his house for lunch instead of going out for pizza or something. Apparently his mother has taken his baby sisters shopping for new clothes in the city today.

Apparently Luke has baby sisters.

"How old are they?" I ask, looking around the van.

"Almost three," Luke says. I screw up my face in concentration as I try to figure out the math.

"Are you wondering whether one of my parents is remarried?" Luke asks with a laugh.

"Sort of," I confess. "It's a pretty huge age difference."

"Yeah, it is," Luke says. "My parents had me young."

"And they decided to have more kids later?"

"Yep," Luke says. "They divorced and remarried each other. Then had the twins."

I must still have a funny look on my face, because Luke keeps talking.

"I know it's weird. Want to hear the saga?"

"Yes," I say enthusiastically.

"Okay," Luke says, smiling. "So, we lived in Chicago when I was born. My parents were high school sweethearts. They got married young, right after graduation. Can you imagine?" he asks, but doesn't let me answer.

"Anyway, they had me when they were twenty-five or something. They were superpoor, so we lived in my grandparents' basement. My dad was in law school and my mom took care of me and worked nights to help pay for it. I guess they were pretty happy despite the no-money thing.

"After school my dad got recruited by a big law firm in New York. We moved there when I was around five or so."

"You lived in New York? That's so cool," I say, remembering the city from visits I'll have as an adult. I can't wait to go.

"Yeah, it was. I mean, I was young, but I remember a lot of it. My mom used to take me around the city. It was really fun. You know how some childhood memories just stick with you?"

"Yeah," I lie, trying to plaster a nostalgic look on my face. Luke pauses and smiles at me. He looks like he wants to ask something, but he doesn't. Instead, he continues his story.

"Anyway, the fun didn't last long. Dad made partner and my parents started fighting because he spent a lot of time at work. Like, *a lot*. I don't remember him being home much for a few years."

At least you remember him at all, I think.

Luke exits the freeway and turns right, toward the newer housing development across the highway from mine. I am happy to discover how close we live to each other.

Luke goes on. "So when I was about ten, they got a divorce. For two years, I didn't see my dad at all. He sent cards on my birthday and stuff..."

Cringe.

"...and I know he paid child support. We moved to Boston. My mom took a job at a furniture store. She worked a ton and so I spent the summers with my aunt and uncle."

Luke pauses again, as if he's waiting for me to say

something. Unsure how to respond, I look back until he is forced to return his eyes to the road. He continues.

"Then one day Dad showed up with flowers and begged Mom to take him back. Eventually, she did, and he took a job in Boston at a smaller firm and came home at five thirty every night. It was like New York had never happened.

"It was all pretty weird, but that's my parents. Then one day they shock me with news that they're having twins."

"Wow," I say when he's finished.

"I know, sorry. That was really long and boring," Luke says.

"No, not at all. It sounds like a movie."

Luke laughs and says, "Oh, I'm sure we all have our movie dramas," in a way that makes me think he can see into my soul.

"What about your parents?" he asks casually.

"My mom sells real estate," I say, eyes on the houses we're passing.

"What about your dad? What does he do?"

"I don't know," I say quietly. Luke glances at me.

"Sorry for bringing it up," he says.

"It's no big deal," I lie. In truth, it's a very big deal, particularly today, but it's nothing I need to share with a potential boyfriend who seems to play no part in my future. I'm relieved when we reach Luke's house. Luke's very new, very large house.

We go in, and after a quick tour of the main level, Luke fixes turkey sandwiches in the kitchen while I scan a mantel in the library bursting with framed photos of him and his little sisters. I feel a little twinge of jealousy at the sight of the happy siblings.

A particular photo of Luke when he looks to be eleven or twelve catches my attention, then magnetically draws it back the first few times I look away. In it, he's clearly going through a tough-guy fashion phase. I can't stop looking at it.

Finally, I focus on shots of his baby sisters.

"They're adorable," I say about the little girls when Luke brings in lunch.

"Yeah, they really are. You should see them in real life. They say the most hilarious stuff." Luke is beaming, and the thought of him serving as older brother to these two precious ladies feels right. "Anyway, you'll meet them sometime," he adds. "Here you go," he says, offering me a plate.

"I didn't know you were on a crew team," I say before taking a bite of the best turkey sandwich on earth.

He frowns, and I consider that he might have shared that with me already. Instead, he replies, "I need to keep you away from the photos."

"It's cute," I mumble through bread and turkey, admiring a photo of Luke and his teammates. He looks oddly out of place among the Ivy-bound prepsters, but strangely at ease just the same.

"Ha-ha," he replies sarcastically, and then smiles. "I'm not really into team sports, but crew was pretty fun. You have no idea what cold is until you've been dunked in the Charles River at six in the morning."

We share a laugh and then finish our lunches before Luke gives me a guided tour of the rest of the house. It's gorgeous, and with every new room, I search for traces of him.

Luke does his homework here. Luke watches TV there. Luke plays video games here. Luke eats dinner there.

Upstairs, there are four bedrooms bordering a U-shaped balcony that overlooks the main entryway. In one corner is the master bedroom; closest to it is the twins' bedroom. Next is the guest bedroom.

And then, we approach Luke's room.

My heart races a bit as I take in the dark wood and deep blue walls, which stand in stark contrast to the lightness of the rest of the house. I can see a well-worn guitar leaning against a low chair in the corner. A massive oil painting of a girl's ear rests against the wall. It's strange and beautiful at the same time, and I can't help but wonder who the ear belongs to. Does Luke want to paint my ear?

The covers are thrown in a modest attempt at making the bed, and I find myself wanting to run over and smell the pillows.

Somehow, I manage not to act like a total stalker.

We're tight on time, so I don't get much farther than

the doorway, and too soon, Luke is gently guiding me away from the only place I care to be at this second.

"We should go," he says softly, placing his hand on my back. "I don't want to get you into trouble."

I reluctantly agree, but as we make our way back down the grand staircase and out to the minivan, I feel an unmistakable pull from his bedroom.

There is just so much *Luke* in that room. I want more of it.

We drive back to school in comfortable silence and walk inside hand in hand. Just before parting ways in the middle of the commons, Luke turns to face me.

"Want to go out on Saturday night?"

"Yes," I say, maybe before he's even finished his question. I grin at him and he laughs at me.

And then he moves closer.

I hold my breath, considering that Luke might kiss me right here in the middle of the commons. Just as I'm deciding whether or not I can kiss with an audience, Luke, staring intently into my eyes, raises a hand toward my face. Slowly, softly, he rubs his thumb along my jawbone. I'm hypnotized by the most perfect kind of touch. Oddly, it feels even more intimate than a kiss.

"Talk to you later," Luke whispers, before breaking the trance and heading off in the direction of his next class.

"Bye," I breathe after him.

I stand still, relishing the moment. Then, just before I

turn to float to History, a familiar outfit catches my eye. At the other end of the vast common area, Jamie stands in front of the soda machine, staring at me.

I wave and she waves back, but there is something missing in her simple gesture. I consider going over and talking to her. But before my feet can move, Jamie turns and leaves.

14

"Jamie?"

"Hi! Why are you answering like that?"

"I'm just surprised that you're calling, I guess," I admit.

"Why?" Jamie plays dumb.

"You seemed upset today," I say softly.

"I don't know what you're talking about." I imagine the guilty look on her face on the other end of the phone. I can hear it in her voice, and that's enough for me. I'm moving on.

"So what's up?"

"Not much," she says. "Had dinner, watched some TV."

"Me, too."

"Did you say anything to your mom about the stuff you found?"

"What? No!" I practically shout into the phone. "I can't talk to her about that," I add at a lower volume.

"I hear you," Jamie says in a way that annoys me. Jamie's mom will never be sneaky like mine. She'll support Jamie through everything.

"Anyway, I did it," she says.

"Did what?" I ask.

"Ugh, your messed-up memory is so annoying sometimes," she says with a heavy sigh. "I met Ted after school."

And then, I remember.

I remember the relationship that will destroy a marriage, ruin a career, and break my best friend's heart. I recall notes about trying to talk her out of it, and more notes about trying to ignore it.

I remember the future when it all plays out, and suddenly I feel sick to my stomach. Jamie is stubborn, but I should have tried harder.

"Oh, Jamie. Are you okay?"

"Okay? Are you serious? I'm better than okay. He's amazing."

I can't help but wonder if this is in response to Jamie seeing me with Luke.

"Jamie, I just think you need to really consider what you're doing. This is a big deal." I'm trying to sound like a concerned friend and not a parent, but it's coming out the other way around.

"I thought you'd be happy for me."

"J, I want you to be happy. I just don't think this is right. I'm really worried about you."

"Well, don't be," Jamie snaps.

I know she's pissed, and yet, I have to keep trying. I ignore the notes that told me never to tell Jamie about her future.

"He's not going to leave his wife, and you'll just end up hurt. You'll even try to..."

"SHUT UP, LONDON!" Jamie shouts into the phone. "I told you not to tell me anything, and you wrote it down, so I know you know. Don't even try to pretend you don't."

"Fine," I say forcefully. "I won't tell you. But you don't have to remember the future to know that a grown man only wants one thing from a high school girl."

"Don't be a bitch, London."

"I won't, if you stop acting like a slut."

We're both silent, and I immediately want to suck the biting words back into my mouth. But it's too late. My memory is right: Jamie and I won't talk again for a while after this. Still, I try to fix the situation.

"J, I just worry about you."

"Well, you don't have to worry anymore. We're done."

Click.

15

10/27 (Wed.)

Clothes:
—Black cardigan with yellow tank underneath
—Faded Levi's

School:
—Math test (read chapters 5 and 6 before school)
—Downloaded a couple cool logo samples for graphic design project (in backpack)
—Finish English essay & print before Friday

Drama:

Check out Dark Memory file on computer. I think it might be Dad's funeral. Can't deal with how unfair that is! Almost asked Mom about him today, but decided it was a bad idea (see envelope of stuff she's hidden from me). WHY?? I want to meet him before anything happens.

Jamie is seriously <u>pissed</u>! She ignored me in Spanish (notes say she has all week), then came over after school for a borrowed clothes swap like we were breaking up. Barely spoke to me, then ripped the BFF poster in half!! I feel bad but this is crazy.

Bright side:

Luke and I have a date on Sat. night!! Unfortunately, we didn't talk much in study hall today. He was sketching a giant ear (?) most of the time and then he had to go help his mom at lunch. Think he was about to kiss me before he left! Maybe Sat.

16

"Have I ever changed something that was supposed to happen?" I ask my mom as we pull into the parking lot before school. My head is heavy and it's only 7:24 in the morning.

"What do you mean?"

"The future," I say, wishing for one second she could read my mind so that I didn't have to explain it. "My memories. Have I ever changed a memory?"

"Hmm, let me think," she says, pondering the thought a little too long. Finally, she's got something. "You skipped Jamie's thirteenth birthday party."

"Why?"

"You remembered that you were going to break your

nose," she says with a chuckle. Not funny, I think, but I stay quiet and listen. "It was a pool party at the rec center, out on the deck. There were sliding glass doors and you remembered running full force into one of them. So you skipped the party."

"And what happened?" I ask.

"You missed out on the fun and you broke your nose later that year when you tripped over a stray dog that you brought home."

We're idle in the drop-off area, and I need to get out now. She looks over and touches the tip of a nose that looked perfectly fine to me in the mirror this morning.

"So, really, I didn't change anything?" I ask, part dejected and part annoyed. Frankly, I'm having a hard time not asking her why she's been lying to me all my life, as this morning's notes reported.

"I guess not," my mom says. When I exhale loudly, she adds, "That's not to say that you couldn't, you know. Maybe you just didn't in that situation. What's wrong, London?"

"I just feel sick," I say, because right now, I really do.

Another parent gives her car horn a gentle tap to politely ask us to move along. My mom glances in the rearview mirror, then looks at me earnestly.

"You know, London, the thing is, unless you told me about it or wrote it down, you wouldn't really know that you were making changes to your future, even if you were. Does that make sense?"

I take a moment to consider her statement. Say that

right now, I remember that tomorrow I'll be hit by a bus. I don't tell my mom about it or write it down tonight, so tomorrow morning that knowledge is lost completely. But tomorrow, I take a different route to school and unknowingly avoid the bus-hitting incident. Then, I've changed my future without knowing it.

I genuinely smile for the first time this morning.

"It makes perfect sense," I say as I release my seat belt and open the door. I wave good-bye, rush inside, and head to my first class.

Barely inside the locker room, I'm accosted by Page Thomas.

"Have you asked him yet?" she says, standing awkwardly in her baggy sportswear.

I can see a costume in Page's locker instead of street clothes. I'm dressed in a black crewneck sweater, a black denim skirt, and orange and black striped tights that I found in my dresser. Not a costume, but festive just the same.

Page stares at me, arms crossed, as if it's my duty to seal her romantic fate. For a glimmer of a second, I consider telling her the truth. But then, I think of Brad Thomas and what he'll do to her. I think of her public rejection. I think of the sadness in her when it happens.

And then I think of myself.

Underneath it all, I can't deny that I want to try to change something small to find out whether I might be able to change something big.

With all this in mind, rather than telling Page Thomas the truth—that I never actually spoke to Brad—I turn to face the girl in the baggy sportswear and spew a lie right to her face.

"Page," I say, feigning sympathy. "I'm so sorry, but apparently Brad Thomas is gay."

17

"Bye," I call to my mom before closing the front door and joining Luke on the porch.

This is it: our first date.

I pored through the notes all day, giggling and gasping right up until the moment I started getting ready. That took an hour, and then I spent the next one toning it down to make it look effortless.

He's late, but I don't mind. He's here.

Luke directs me to the maroon minivan in the driveway (which I'm glad my notes warned me about, because otherwise I'd be concerned). He holds the door open for me in a way that's more natural than forced. He seems to be a gentleman, probably the product of polite parents.

We settle into our seats and strap seat belts across our bodies. "Sorry I'm late," he says.

"It's fine," I say.

"I got caught up in a painting," he explains as he turns the ignition and adjusts the heat. "I lost track of time."

Annoyance creeps up on me. He was painting? I take a deep breath and shove it away. He's here now.

"How are you?" he asks, so intimately that I want to grab him. I'm completely over his lateness.

"I'm fine," I say, smiling. "How about you?"

"Better now," he says, expertly backing out of the driveway onto the quiet street.

"Do I smell pizza?" I ask, suddenly salivating. Luke glances in my direction and then forward again.

"Sorry," he says. "I just picked some up for my family before I left."

"Oh," I say, and shrug to myself as Luke shifts the van into drive and accelerates.

The radio plays quietly as Luke navigates the streets of my development like he's lived here for years. Soon enough, we're barreling north on one of the two highways that run in and out of town.

"What happened to the movie?" I ask. He had outlined a dinner and movie date for my mom, but I don't care where we go. I don't mind if I stare at a blank wall, as long as I do it in Luke's presence.

"Don't worry, I didn't lie to your mom," he says cryptically.

"I wasn't worried, and it's okay if you did," I say, looking out at the clear, cold night.

Luke drives and I ride north and north and north of town, and for a fleeting second, I wonder whether I'm that girl in horror movies who walks toward the monster instead of running to safety. I'm breezily allowing this cute guy I don't remember to take me to the boondocks. Then, as quickly as it arrived, I push the thought away. There is nothing monstrous about Luke Henry. There is nothing frightening about the boy I know from my notes. I feel completely safe in this van that smells like pizza.

I watch the sky as we drive, and the farther we get from the city, the more stars appear. "Do you even know where you're going?" I ask, not minding if we get lost. "Didn't you just move here?"

"I scoped out our destination this afternoon," he admits.

"How very organized of you," I say, settling back into the seat and feeling totally at ease. I'm completely calm as Luke turns off the highway onto a frontage road, takes a right onto a smaller residential street, and turns right onto a dirt road that winds up a small hill into blackness.

I feel the safest I will feel in years as this stranger eases his mother's minivan off the gravel and drives slowly across the prairie to the edge of a small hill.

Luke parks directly in front of a NO TRESPASSING sign on the barbed-wire fence that keeps us from driving off the incline. He kills the engine and the headlights along with it. I take in the twinkling, scattered town below, sprawling across more than twenty miles of land, just because it can.

"Cool," I say.

"Yeah, I thought so," he says, eyes straight ahead. I like that he likes this town. It's not for everyone, but it will always be a little part of me.

"So, you've never been up here before?"

Good question, I think. "Um, no," I reply. "In fact, I have no idea where we are."

Luke takes his eyes off the landscape for the first time and settles on me. His hands are still resting lightly on the steering wheel. "You're pretty trusting, you know. I could be a murderer."

"Yes, you could be, but I doubt it." I say, transfixed by his pale eyes. "I feel too safe with you."

"You are," he says sweetly. He pauses for a few moments and I think he might lean over and kiss me, but he doesn't.

"Okay," he says louder, hitting his hands lightly on the steering wheel. "Let's get this party started. You hungry?"

"Yes, but I don't think anyone delivers out here," I say, scanning the barren land around us.

"Never fear, I've got it covered. Just a minute." Luke pops the back door, gets out, and disappears behind the van. I turn around to see what he's doing and realize that the middle row of seats is missing. On the third row, there are two throw pillows that look like they were taken from someone's couch; a soft knitted blanket folded neatly on the seat; and a small cooler on top of the blanket.

Luke spies me checking out his setup and smiles sheepishly when our eyes meet. My stomach spins at the sight of the dimple on his right cheek.

He closes the door with a light thud. Instead of getting back in the driver's seat, Luke opens the automatic sliding door on the far side of the van and climbs in. He's carrying what looks like a pizza delivery sleeve in his right hand and a plastic bag in his left.

"Liar!" I say playfully.

"Come on back," he instructs with a laugh.

Instead of attempting to gracefully climb between our seats, I get out of the van and enter through the sliding door on my side. Crouched down, I walk to the back of the vehicle and sit next to Luke, who has cleared the blanket and the cooler from the third row and propped a pillow on the seatback for me to lean against. From some secret compartment, he retrieves a remote control.

"Whoops," he says as he gets up and scoots to the front of the van. He reaches up to the dashboard and turns the ignition, fiddles with the heater and some other controls, then returns to our seat. I hadn't noticed the dropdown DVD player until now; it illuminates the backseat. A copyright warning is our nightlight as Luke pulls a miraculously warm pizza from the sleeve (apparently he "borrowed" it), retrieves paper plates and napkins from the sack, and grabs sodas from the cooler.

I recognize the movie from the first five notes of its sound track. As the signature opener of Star Wars scrolls up the tiny screen, I scoot closer to Luke Henry on our make-shift couch in the middle of nowhere. I am the happiest I'll be in years.

"I love this movie," I whisper.

"Yeah," he smiles, still looking at the screen.

"Yeah, what?" I ask.

"I thought you might." Luke looks at me like he can see into my soul, and all of a sudden I feel naked. Breaking the tension, I reach for the pizza at my feet and begin eating. Luke follows suit, and between the two of us, the whole thing is gone quickly.

Full and content, we watch the movie in silence. Half-way through, I pull the blanket over my legs. Someone texts Luke but he doesn't answer; he turns the ringer off and tosses the phone to the front seat. He puts his arm around my shoulders, and we snuggle together like we've known each other forever.

After the movie, Luke makes his way to the front of the van, explaining that he should turn off the car for a little bit to conserve gas.

"I don't want to get us stranded out here," he explains.

"I wouldn't mind," I reply.

"I wouldn't, either," he says seriously. "But I think your mom might." Instead of rejoining me, Luke pulls open the moonroof and asks me to hand him the pillows. He lines them up against the backs of the driver's and pas-senger seats and lies down with his head on one.

"Come here?" he says, more as a question than a

command. The van has grown cold quickly, so I drag the blanket with me as I scoot to the forward section and lie down parallel to Luke. We settle the blanket over both of us, tucking it in around our bodies to trap the heat.

Luke and I stare straight up through the large window at the winter sky, overcrowded with stars. My teeth begin to chatter and my body starts shaking, but it's not the cold. Luke moves closer to me and grabs my hand under the covers.

"This is nice," he says softly, after a few moments of silence.

"Yes, it is," I say quietly.

"Like we've known each other for a while, right?" he asks.

"Uh-huh," I mumble, scooting closer to Luke's warm shoulder.

"Want my theory?" Luke asks, carefully rolling onto his side to face me. His eyes look mischievous, like he's got a great secret to tell.

"Yes, please," I say, still on my back but facing him instead of the stars now.

"Reincarnation."

"Reincarnation?"

"Yeah, you know what that is, right?" he asks.

"Of course I do. I'm not dumb. I'm just wondering what that has to do with us."

"Well, my theory is that we were married in some

past life. Maybe I was a great king and you were my queen and we were killed by an angry mob."

"What did we do to make the mob so angry that they wanted to kill us?" I tease.

Luke laughs and continues. "All right, forget that. Maybe we were just average people living sometime, someplace. Just elsewhere."

"Elsetime."

"That's not even a word," he says, sidetracked.

"I know. I just made it up. Go on."

"Okay, fine, we were married elsetime. Anyway, we died of whatever you die from, let's say natural causes. But we were in love, so our souls keep finding each other in whatever forms our bodies take."

"Are you Hindu or something?" I ask, avoiding the fact that my stomach is in knots from hearing his beautiful theory.

"No, we used to be Catholic. But I did have a religion class at my last school that exposed us to different ideas. I think the concept of reincarnation is a good one."

"If you're Catholic, shouldn't you believe in heaven and hell and all that?"

"I said I used to be Catholic," he replies.

"No heaven then, huh?" I press on.

"Who knows until we experience it? I think that heaven and reincarnation are both ways of making us feel better about what happens to people's souls after death. I hope at least one of them is true. I don't like to think about being worm food."

"Yeah, I don't really like to think of death at all," I reply truthfully.

We're both quiet for a few minutes, and then Luke breaks the silence. "I think you're supposed to save the death discussion until at least the third date." We chuckle halfheartedly and Luke rolls onto his back again.

Trying to lighten the mood, I ask, "What were our names?"

"Our names?" Luke says, sounding confused.

"Yes, our names. Elsetime. When we were madly in love and married and all that."

"It sounds so cheesy when you say it like that." Luke looks away for a few seconds, and I imagine that he's blushing, but I can't be sure.

"No," I say quickly. "I like it. Don't be embarrassed."

He looks back into my eyes and we're locked there for a few moments. And then, before I can worry about what he's doing, Luke leans over and kisses me. Barely there at first, then more purposeful, the kiss is soft and electric at the same time. It's so perfect that, before it's over, I'm heartbroken that I won't remember it.

When we part, Luke's eyes stay on mine. The moment is more intense than even he knows; I look away.

"Are you okay?" he asks. "Was that bad?"

Quickly, I meet his gaze again. "No!" I say a little too

loudly. "Not at all. It was amazing." I'm glad to be in the dark; I can feel my face flush.

"Good," Luke says. "Because I've wanted to do that for a while."

"Well, I'm glad you did," I reply with a grin. Maybe it's the acknowledgment of the situation, but at once I feel silly. Luke might, too: he eases onto his back again, careful to leave room for me to cuddle close.

There's an awkward silence again.

Until I throw a rock through it.

"So elsetime . . . I think my name was Heloise. Or Elizabeth. No, I've got it. I was Caroline."

Luke waits a beat, and then joins the game. "That's a good one," he responds earnestly. "And I was Benjamin."

"Or William," I interrupt.

"Oh yeah, that's good, too. I was William. I was a stonemason."

"Of course you were. And I was a housewife raising our three children: Eliza, Mathilda, and . . ."

"Rex, after our pet dinosaur."

"REX?" I screech. All of the happy nervousness jumps out of me at once; I burst out laughing and can't stop. I am delirious. Luke laughs with me for a minute and then calms himself and stares in awe as I curl into a ball and nearly hyperventilate. By the time I've composed myself, I have tears streaming down my cheeks, and my stomach muscles ache.

"That funny, huh?"

Residual giggles sneak out of me as I unfold myself and smooth the blanket back across my legs. "Pretty funny," I agree. "Or maybe I'm just easily amused."

"Cheap date," he teases. I lean over and playfully punch him with my left hand, which he grabs and holds for safekeeping.

"You're surprising," I say, looking to the sky.

"How so?" he asks.

"Most guys don't make up stories like that," I say quietly, thinking of the boys and men I will encounter in my lifetime. "Especially not guys who look like you."

"Well, most girls who look like you are prom queens," Luke says, matching my tone. "But you seem to avoid the spotlight. You have one good friend, and you do your own thing. I like that about you." He kisses my knuckles and it sends a spark through me.

"Where did we live?" I ask softly, gently removing my hand so that I can lie flat and get comfortable. I scoot even closer to his side, if that's possible. "Let's see...I believe we lived in...Ireland." I've answered my own question.

"Oh, right," Luke agrees, clearly okay heading back to make-believe. "And we farmed potatoes."

"We were busy," I murmur, feeling exhausted. The emotions, the laughter, the warmth of Luke's body, it's all weighing me down now.

"Yes, we were. Very, very busy."

"I had red hair," I continue, so comfortable I feel like

I'm in my own bed. Of course, Luke wouldn't be there with me, so I'm glad I'm here.

"You have red hair now," he says.

"I think I'll always have red hair."

"I hope so. It's one of the best things about you." Luke's words are garbled and I'm spellbound by the even tone of his voice and the vast blackness of the universe above.

"Thanks." I speak in a barely audible tone.

Luke's breath is even now, and mine falls into step with his. I am thankful for this day, this boy beside me, and this blanket keeping us warm.

A distant question forms in the depths of my mind.

What time is it?

The question is fleeting, flitting, pushed aside by a more prevalent and wonderful thought: I think I'm falling in love.

No, I know I am.

I'm falling in love with Luke.

I close my eyes from the sheer mass of it all, just for a moment.

For a few moments.

For a while.

And now, I'm in Ireland.

I'm in the Ireland I've seen in movies, at least. Standing in a gargantuan green field with a short stone wall marking perimeters too far off to reach, I know this is our land, Luke's and mine. The tiny stone cottage behind us with the smoke billowing from the chimney is ours, too.

Beside me, Luke wears a thick ivory wool sweater and a plaid scarf, and he smokes a pipe.

Since when does Luke smoke a pipe?

More important, what are we doing in Ireland?

Most important, why is that Tyrannosaurus rex charging toward us, teeth bared and hungry?

Oh no.

Oh NO!

No no no no no!!!!!

This can't be happening.

Somehow, from deep in my consciousness, I realize that I'm asleep. I know this sweater-wearing, smoking, Irish Luke is not the real Luke, the one that already I can't remember. The thought of him is barely out of reach, but it's gone nonetheless. Like something you were going to say but forgot and can't quite grasp again.

I reach into the pockets of my dream apron and search frantically for the note that I haven't left myself. It's not there in my dream; it will not be there when I awaken.

There is no note.

There will be no memory.

Real Luke is gone.

18

"WHERE AM I?" I shout, terrified.

I sit up and pull the blanket to my chest. Whose blanket is this?

I take in my surroundings.

I'm in a van.

I'm in a van with a strange guy.

I strain my neck to peek out the window and realize that I'm in the middle of nowhere. In a van! Rapists drive vans! Wondering if I've been violated, I concentrate on my private parts for any indication of wrongdoing. The parts seem to have remained private, but I can't be sure.

Hysteria creeps through my veins and I scream again, louder this time. "WHERE AM I?"

The stranger startles awake.

"Huh?" he croaks, staring at me like I'm crazy. He blinks his eyes a couple of times, and then shakes his head like he's waking from a bad dream.

"What is going—" He sits up and looks out the window. "No!" he shouts. "Oh, no! This is baaaaaaad. It's light out!"

Obviously, I think but don't vocalize. I don't want to poke the bear.

"What time is it?" he asks under his breath. He is furiously trying to untangle himself from his half of the blanket I'm holding, so I let it go. He succeeds, and pushes a button to open the sliding door next to him. He hops out of the van, closes the sliding door, and throws himself into the driver's seat. In moments, the van roars to life.

"We gotta go," he says, adjusting the rearview mirror. "Are you riding back there?" he asks.

I consider that it might be easier to jump from the passenger seat if need be, so I move to the front of the van. I keep my hand firmly wrapped around the door handle as mystery boy backs away from a barbed-wire fence and toward a dirt road.

"London, are you okay?" he asks, once we've turned onto a paved residential road. At least he knows my name. And he looks to be my age. It's possible that I managed to willingly get myself into this situation, and then forgot to write a note.

"London?" he asks, looking at me with eyes I didn't

know anyone other than movie stars possessed. His voice sounds almost fearful. This calms me slightly, which is good, because I think I'm approaching a major panic attack.

"I'm fine," I answer, before looking away from him and out the window.

"I'm so sorry," he says. When I don't respond, he adds, "Your mom must be really strict, huh? I hope you aren't in serious trouble."

We're silent as we ride, and then we're turning off the highway toward my housing development. My shoulders begin to relax with the realization that this stranger is at least driving me home. The terror has subsided. I must know this person; I just need to get home and ask my mom who he is or look in my spiral notebooks to figure it out.

And then, new terror sets in when I consider that sleeping in the middle of nowhere in vans with strange boys isn't something my mother will condone. Nor is coming home at — what time is it, anyway? — 7:14 in the morning. As the boy rounds the street corner to my house, I can almost see it breathing with motherly rage.

We're barely into the driveway before the front door flings open and my mom is rushing to meet me. The car hasn't stopped before she begins tugging at the door handle.

"Oh, man," the boy whispers as he struggles to put the van in park so that the automatic locks will release. "I'm so sorry, London," he says once again, and I feel bad for him this time.

"Both of you, in the house!" my mom barks at me and the stranger. He tentatively turns off the engine and unbuckles his seat belt. I mimic his movements and follow him and my mom inside. My mom storms through the front entryway to the living room and stops abruptly in the center of the room.

"Sit!" she orders when we hover on the fringe. I take a seat on the far edge of the chocolate leather couch, and the boy sits in the middle. He leaves a decent amount of space between us but doesn't wimp out by sitting at the opposite end. The guy has guts.

"First of all, let me just state the obvious," my mom begins, with measured restraint. "You're both grounded." I wonder how my mom has the authority to ground Mr. Mystery, but she continues. "I've been on the phone all night with your mother and father, Luke."

Luke? Nice name.

Mom goes on. "It's unfortunate that I had to meet new members of our community under these circumstances. But I think that you'll find your father's current state even more unfortunate. He was out looking for the two of you all night. He is not happy."

Luke groans next to me and hangs his head.

The berating continues. "I'll call them on your way home so they know you're safe. But first, will one of you please tell me where on earth you were this whole night? I tried to call and text a million times."

I take out my cell and find five texts and eight missed calls. "I turned it off," I mutter, looking down. As I replace the phone in my pocket, Mom folds her arms across her chest and the room grows silent. I look at Luke. He raises his eyebrows expectantly, as if he thinks I'm going to explain the situation to my mother. As if I *can* explain the situation to my mother. He has no idea.

I am mute.

"Seriously?" he whispers at me harshly before turning to face my mom.

"We were out past Old Fox Road, just north of town," he says. "I planned this whole dinner-and-a-movie thing. My minivan has a DVD player and we ate pizza and looked at the stars. It was no big deal ... until I guess we fell asleep. I'm really sorry, Mrs. Lane.

"What?" he hisses at me when he glances my way and sees my openmouthed stare.

I can't believe I missed what might have been my best date ever.

I turn to my mom, mouth still slightly ajar, and the ice melts. I see in her eyes the realization. She understands now that I don't remember the evening. Keeping up the façade for Luke's benefit, she asks, "Is that true, London?" Her look tells me to agree.

"Yes," I breathe, finding myself desperate to be alone with Luke and have him retell every minute of the night. Judging by his expression of sour lemons with a dash of confusion, I doubt he's interested in reliving the fun just yet. I doubt that I told him anything about my faulty wiring. I doubt it, but I can't be sure.

My mom speaks again. "Okay, then. Because I trust my daughter, and because you seem like you come from a nice family, Luke, I choose to believe that this was an honest mistake, and we'll leave it at that. I don't love the fact that the two of you were so far out of town alone, but I can't say that I didn't explore the outskirts of the area a time or two myself when I was your age."

My mom smiles, and Luke's expression is now confused. He doesn't understand why this woman has just turned compassionate. She puts on her Tough Mom hat again and adds, in a harsher tone, "But you're still grounded. Luke, you'd better get home; your parents are worried."

With that, she leaves the room and heads to the kitchen. I know that this is her way of letting me say good-bye to Luke without her watchful eye on us.

I walk him to the door. Before he leaves, he turns and eyes me skeptically.

"What happened back there?" he asks.

"I'm so sorry," I begin, because I am. "I just froze. I've never done anything like this before." I say it because I think it's true.

"And I have? It's not like I'm some degenerate or something. My parents are going to kill me."

"I'm really sorry," I say again, stepping closer to him.

He grabs my hand and smiles down at me through his thick eyelashes, and my heart sputters.

"Was it worth it?" he asks seriously.

"Yes," I say, looking up at him. Standing here, holding the hand of this gorgeous being even for these few moments, is worth every bit of it. "Do you think so?" I ask in return.

"Definitely," he says, brushing a strand of hair from my face. He bends down and lightly skims my lips with his, then whispers in my ear, "See you soon, prom queen."

19

It's 2:39 in the morning.

My heart is racing. I'm sweating and chugging water and feeling helpless.

I turn on the lamp, grab the pen, and, at the end of a very, very long note about boys and darkness and adulterers and liars, I write this simple addendum:

It's not Dad.

Then somehow, amazingly, I will myself to sleep.

MONDAY

1/30 (Sun.)

Outfit:
    —Faded Levi's
    —Red sweatshirt

School:
    —Bring book for English
    —Review drills for Spanish quiz before school
    —Buy SAT prep book

Important stuff:

Jamie. Still not speaking. Try asking her to help with finding Dad (read back and look in the big envelope in the desk). Also, try to think of a plan to help end her tragic relationship.

Mom. See the big envelope mentioned above.

Luke. SUPERHOT BOYFRIEND! He'll be there before school with coffee and food of some sort; don't worry about breakfast. Dating almost three and a half months. Supergood kisser. Flip through notes and check out the photos all over the room. See Saturday's note about a party at his friend Adam's house. Today, we went to the movie Elephant Bride and it was really stupid but the day was fun anyway. I beat him at a fighting video game before the movie. I was the Red Warrior.

Held hands the whole movie and shared popcorn; he called me a popcorn hog. Went to his house after and he played his guitar for me for a while until Mom called and told me to come home for dinner. We kissed before I got out of the car. Yum. Oh, he drives a minivan—don't hold it against him.

20

What I'm really thinking right now is "whoa." What comes out of my mouth, miraculously, is a simple, sultry, "Hey."

"Hey yourself," he says, backlit and beautiful, standing on my porch with a lidded coffee cup in his hand. I can see his breath in the frigid air as it escapes his mouth.

There is something overwhelming about the moment. His unwavering gaze, effortless smile, and obvious ease, combined with the February sunrise, make me feel like my legs might give out underneath me.

"Ready?" he asks gently.

"Yep," I say, in a measured tone that I'm surprised I'm capable of using. I follow him from the porch to the mini-van idling in the driveway.

I thought I was prepared.

This morning, I read months of notes. I flipped through dozens of photos.

But Luke in real life is something else.

Luke in real life is something no amount of notes could prepare me for. My living, breathing boyfriend is amazing.

Trying to act as if I remember being here before, I slide into the passenger seat and buckle my belt. Once I'm settled, Luke gestures to a coffee waiting for me in the passenger cup holder.

"There are muffins in the console," he says casually as he backs out of the driveway. I open the compartment between us to find breakfast from what will be my favorite bakery until it goes out of business in a few years.

I know from notes that this has become our ritual: Luke driving me to school each day, often surprising me with morning treats. But thanks to my lack of proper memory, it feels like a first for me today, and I love it.

"Jamie ever call you back yesterday?" Luke asks as he drives. My notes didn't say I called her, but they would have if she'd called back.

"No," I say, pretty sure that I'm telling the truth.

"Bummer."

Too soon, we're pulling into the student lot. Even though we're one of the first cars there, Luke turns into a space in the back row.

"Easy escape," he says when I look at him quizzically.

He puts the gearshift in park but leaves the engine running and the heat pumping. I wonder whether Luke always parks in the back and make a mental note to include that tonight so I don't wonder again.

"Are you cold?" he asks.

"No, I'm fine. If anything, I'm hot in this jacket."

He turns down the blower.

"Your hair looks good like that," he says, as easily as someone I've been dating for a while might. He takes a slow sip of his coffee, and I find myself wishing my own nearly empty cup would magically refill itself.

I grab a smooth strand of hair. I must have flat-ironed it last night; I didn't wash it this morning.

"Thanks," I say, gazing into his blue eyes.

"So, what's new?" he asks.

I have no idea, so I talk about my best friend some more. "I'm worried about Jamie," I begin cryptically, hoping to draw out information if I've already discussed this particular issue with Luke. According to my notes, I haven't. Then again, notes could be wrong.

"How come?" Luke asks innocently, taking another drink. The parking lot is starting to fill around us, but we are in our own world.

"Can I tell you something in confidence?" I ask.

"Of course. You know you can trust me, London."

I do know that, I think to myself.

"Okay," I begin. "You can't tell anyone."

"Of course," he says, as if it's a given.

I sit for a moment, looking into Luke's expectant eyes, trying to think of a way to buffer what I'm going to say. Instead, I finally just blurt it out. "Jamie is having an affair with a teacher. A *married* teacher."

Luke doesn't make a sound, but his jaw drops slightly, and then he recovers. "Wow," he says, clearly letting the news settle in his brain.

"I tried to talk her out of it, but she's too stubborn to listen," I continue.

"How long has this been going on?" he asks.

"It started around the time we met."

I think I see a speck of hurt flash across his eyes—maybe because I didn't tell him sooner. I'm surprised myself that I haven't, but it's not really my secret to tell. And here now, sharing it anyway, I can't help but feel a bit guilty.

"Which teacher?" Luke asks, and all at once I'm defensive.

"It doesn't matter," I snap.

"Whoa, calm down," he snaps back, making me wonder whether we're going to have our first fight. "Just asking," he says, looking toward the line of cars pulling into the lot.

"Sorry, it's just a sensitive subject. No matter how stupid she is sometimes, Jamie is still my best friend. But I didn't mean to bite your head off." Luke looks back into my eyes and smiles. I can see we're okay, but just to make sure, I add, "It's Mr. Rice."

"Driver's Ed.?" Luke asks. I nod.

"I guess I can see that," Luke says. "He's young and all. At least it's not Mr. Ellis."

"Ew, gross!" I squeal, and we chuckle a little at something that really isn't that funny, but it lightens the mood just the same.

A car parks in the space on Luke's side and two girls get out, looking enviously at him and then scowling at me. As they walk toward the school, I remember that one of them is going to get pregnant at the end of next year. I feel like shouting after her, "Use protection!"

Instead, I keep the conversation going.

"I really don't know what to do. I want to find a way to end their relationship without having Jamie know it was me."

"What, you mean like telling on her?"

"In a way, yes," I say.

"What if she gets in trouble?" he asks softly. Luke drains his coffee cup and I admire his profile.

"I don't want that. But I want it to stop, and Jamie isn't willing to listen to me. In fact, she's not even speaking to me because I told her that I was worried."

"That's a tough one," Luke says sincerely.

"I know. But I'll figure it out. There's got to be a way," I say more to myself than to him.

"I'll help you however I can," he replies, even though I think he knows I was talking to myself, too.

Luke grabs my hand over the center compartment and squeezes it gently. The lot is nearly full now.

"We should go in," he says, sounding disappointed.

"Guess so."

He turns the key and the van is silent. I unbuckle my belt and yank my backpack off the floor in front of my feet. Opening the door, I feel a frigid blast of wind that's in stark contrast to the warmth of the van. I hop out, slam the door, and shiver my way to the front of the car to meet Luke. He looks unfazed.

"Aren't you cold?" I ask.

"Not really," he replies with a shrug. "This is no match for the Charles," he adds, confusing me.

Luke grabs my hand and we walk quickly toward the building. His fingers are calloused, and I wonder if it's from playing guitar.

Halfway through the lot, a car is pulling into one of the few vacant spots. It is a blue four-door sedan that someone's mother might drive. Then I realize that Brad from math is driving it. I wave. He glares at me in return.

What I did to Brad to provoke such disdain, I have no idea. But right now, walking hand in hand with my perfect boyfriend on a sunny, crisp February morning, I don't care about Brad from math.

I don't care about anything at all, except Luke.

"Are you sure I can't switch partners?" Jamie asks Ms. Garcia, none too discreetly. A few of our classmates are staring at me to gauge my reaction.

"Ms. Connor, as I've told you now a half-dozen times,

the partner you *chose* at the beginning of the year is the partner you will have until the end. I don't want to hear another word about it."

Ms. Garcia turns her back on Jamie and starts writing today's class agenda on the whiteboard. Jamie rolls her eyes and trudges back to her desk, which she picks up and plunks down with a loud bang so that it's facing mine.

"Whatever," she mutters as she flops into her seat.

"Hi, J," I say quietly.

"Don't talk to me," she snaps.

"I have to: we have an assignment."

"Then only talk to me in Spanish," she commands.

"*Hola*, Jamie," I say as a joke. She doesn't laugh, opting to roll her eyes again instead. I decide to try a new tack, courtesy of this morning's note.

"I need your help," I say quietly.

"Ask your precious Luke for help," Jamie says loudly, without looking up from our assignment.

"I want to track down my dad."

Jamie flinches a little. Her face softens. Still, her response is bitter: "Google him."

"I tried," I say, without knowing whether I have already.

"You're so transparent," Jamie says, still not looking at me. Not sure what she means, I keep quiet. She sighs, and glares right into my eyes. "You're trying to be all casual, but what you really want is for me to look in my mom's files, right?" she asks, acting put out. And yet, there's a slight softness to her tone; I know I've got her. I can't pinpoint why, but Jamie will always agree to help me. Maybe she figures I'm lost without her. In many ways, I am.

Still, I have no idea what files she's talking about.

"Is that what you're getting at? You want me to look up your dad's information in my mom's legal files?"

The word *legal* makes it click. Jamie's mom will be a divorce lawyer for many years; she probably handled my parents' split. Letting Jamie assume this was my plan all along, I agree.

"You've got me," I say, looking as sheepish as possible without actually feeling that way. "Listen, Jamie, I know you're mad at me and that's fine, but this is important. I don't remember my father at all. You know that. But I want to, and I really need your help. Will you help me?"

Sure, I started the conversation to get Jamie to talk to me, but ultimately, I do want to find my dad. This is the best of both worlds.

"Maybe," Jamie says with a shrug, before refocusing on our assignment.

"Thanks," I whisper across the table island at her.

She ignores me completely for the rest of the class.

21

It's nearly bedtime, and my mom is still out showing houses. Despite being angry with her about what she's been hiding from me, I feel sorry for her for having to be out so late.

Pajama-clad, face washed, and teeth brushed, I retrieve the envelope from my desk drawer. The metal clasp is worn from being opened and closed many times.

I know I found the items inside three and a half months ago. I know I haven't done much with the information.

Emptying the photos and cards onto my bedspread, I slowly, meticulously look through them. Vacation photos, shots in the backyard, holidays. We seem happy.

Looking at my father's face, I can't help but recall the

one memory I have of him from the future. The one that plagues me.

I don't know how I got there. I'm just there, among dozens of mourners experiencing various states of grief.

The brick wall of a man holds back his tears, the younger man with the eighties hairstyle weeps freely. Wet from the rain, stricken with grief, my grandmother crumbles. Beside me, my mother sobs, looking young...vulnerable. A woman in a low-cut dress tries to keep her composure, probably for the sake of the small boy in front of her. Footsteps crowd the muddy path like bread crumbs leading to sadness. Even the stone statue to my left cries for the unknown guest of honor.

I grab my notebook and read back about how I used to think it was my father's funeral. I scoff at myself now, remembering my father arriving late, standing near the back—far from both my mother and his own—and fighting back emotion as the priest I can't hear delivers his message.

I remember willing myself to look away, and seeing the caretaker in the distance, watching us. Watching me.

He's standing in front of a toolshed disguised as a mausoleum and he smiles. It's not an all-out smile; it's the one you use when you want to make someone feel better and smiling is all you can do.

It makes me want to run over and kick him, but I don't. Instead, I stare back until he tosses his cigarette to the ground and saunters inside the shed.

The funeral is over and my father is gone.

Grandma is gone.

Everyone is gone.

And still, even as I turn to follow my mother, I can't see the grave. Try as I might, I can't look down. Somewhere deep inside, I won't let myself remember who is in the hole in the ground.

My thoughts turn to Luke. Is it him?

It can't be him.

Why would my father return after years of absence to attend a funeral for my boyfriend? And my grandmother? It doesn't fit.

It's not Luke.

And yet, when I flip through my spiral-bound substitute for a proper memory again, one truth becomes clear: the darkest memory showed up when he did.

Exhausted from the day and the weight of what's coming, I gather the photos and cards before me into a neat stack and ease them back inside the manila envelope. I fold down the clasp to hold it shut, replace it inside the desk drawer, and set my notes on my nightstand.

After scooting under the covers, I reread the note I left myself, just to make sure everything's there. I add a few details about the memory, and a question: How is Luke involved?

The garage door begins to open; my mom is home. Instead of waiting to say good night, I put the note on my nightstand, click off the lamp, and roll to my side, facing the wall.

Two questions volley back and forth in my mind:

Why can't I remember Luke?

Whose funeral is it?

I'm watching the tennis match with my eyes closed when my mom eeks open my door and whispers, barely audibly, "Good night, sweet London."

Her words are like a sleeping pill; they instantly relax me.

Soon, the tennis match is over.

It's love–love.

No resolution.

22

Walking alone from the locker room to the gymnasium, I am lamenting the fact that it's Thursday. Thursdays are odd-block days: ninety minutes each of my least favorite classes.

No Luke to enjoy.

Then again, no Jamie, either.

I am pondering what to do about Jamie as I lean into the bar across the middle of the massive gym door and set foot onto the gleaming court. It's loud and alive with squeaking sneakers and shouts and pants, and the sensory overload distracts me to the point that I don't see it coming.

Before I have time to jump, duck, or even flinch, my thoughts are obliterated by the weight of a massive rubber ball slamming into the right side of my face. The momentum knocks me sideways and then off balance. I trip over my own feet and fall, without even a smidgen of grace, to the ground.

A loud, embarrassing "oof" comes out of my mouth as my hip hits the floor first, followed by my ribs, and then my head. My right ear rings and my cheek tingles and burns at the same time; hand to cheek, I realize that the rubber ball left a pattern on my skin.

I brush the hair that I haven't had the chance to pull back into a ponytail from my face, then blink once to clear the water from my eyes. With one good ear and only partial vision, I experience the fallout.

Everyone in first-period PE is laughing at me. Some try to hide it; others are actually pointing in my direction. Jerks. I struggle to get back on my feet, but my senses are still off, and it's a lot more difficult than it should be. I feel a little drunk, and, yes, I know what that feels like. I remember it.

Once I finally make it to my feet and the crowd begins to scatter, my eyes catch Page Thomas's. There's a nasty smirk on her face as she quickly looks away. Before I have too much time to dwell on it, a shrill whistle blows. Ms. Martinez commands the room, and I grudgingly join one of two teams.

For the rest of the period, I try to defend myself as best I can through an excruciating "game" that should be banned from high school and general play forever.

It is nothing but pain and humiliation.

It should be avoided at all costs.

It is the reason this morning's note warned: *stay alert first period*.

It is hell on earth.

It is dodgeball.

Hours later, during Ms. Harris's lecture on the hippocampus in Human Anatomy, Ryan Greene keeps glancing at me from across the aisle. My face and ego still sting from this morning, but I'm smiling and I can't stop. It hurts my cheeks, and Ryan is gawking—probably because the hippocampus isn't that exciting—but I don't care.

I saw Luke before class.

"Something funny, London?" Ms. Harris interrupts. She's stopped writing midsentence and is holding the blue dry-erase marker in midair. One of her perfectly curvy hips is popped to the side, and a manicured hand rests there, waiting.

She looks a little like one of the cheerleaders did earlier today. That's concerning, seeing as how Ms. Harris is a teacher and all. Shouldn't she reserve judgment?

Though I'm fairly certain that the majority of them are as bored by the anatomy of the brain as I am, the students in my line of sight now look annoyed at the interruption. More likely, they're just annoyed Ms. Harris turned around.

"London? Is there a joke?" she asks again when I don't

speak. She tosses her dyed red hair and I wonder if she's jealous that mine is real.

"No, Ms. Harris," I say quietly. I try to think of something depressing, but the smile hangs on.

Ms. Harris stares at me, unblinking, for what feels like days. When she seems convinced that I'm either a bad seed or insane, she sighs and turns back to the whiteboard.

The rest of the students right themselves on their stools, and I relax, too. I take a deep breath of stale science-wing air and loosen my grip on the metal table.

My happy moment ruined, I focus on what Ms. Harris is saying, most of it completely snore-inducing. But then, she says something that grabs my interest.

"... possible that we store different types of memories in different parts of our brains."

Intrigued, I sit up a little straighter. I need to hear what she'll say next.

She turns and writes "Types of memories" on the whiteboard. Just as she's underlining her header, the bell rings.

"Class dismissed."

A little over an hour later, Mom is driving in the opposite direction of home, looking determined.

"Where are we going?"

"Out for a snack," she says.

"I'm not hungry," I protest.

"I don't care," she says. "You don't have to eat. But I think we need to spend some time together."

Uh-oh.

Mom pulls into a diner and parks, and we walk inside and seat ourselves as the sign instructs. Once the waitress has taken our drink orders — diet for Mom, regular for me — Mom strikes up a conversation.

"Good day?" she asks.

"No," I answer.

"Why not?"

The waitress delivers our drinks, and my mom unwraps our straws and puts them in the glasses. She takes a sip as she waits for me to respond.

"I got hit in the face with a ball in gym," I answer.

"Are you okay?"

"Yes, I'm fine."

"Good," she says. Another sip. "Anything else?"

"Carley Lynch."

"What did she do this time?" Mom asks.

"She just made some comment about my outfit."

"I love that outfit."

"Me, too," I say.

"You know she's just jealous of you, London."

"No, I don't know, Mom. I don't *remember*."

"Was Jamie there?" my mom asks casually.

"No, of course not," I mutter.

"Still fighting?"

"Obviously," I say, rolling my eyes.

A family scoots into the next booth over, and I watch them settle themselves as my mom speaks in a quieter tone. For that I'm grateful.

"There's no need to get snippy, sweetie. Jamie will come around; she always does. And Carley is jealous because of a boy. Christopher something. They went out for a while and broke up, then you asked him to a dance."

"I asked a boy to a dance?"

"It was a turnabout dance where the girls ask the boys. Jamie talked you into it. Anyway, you weren't interested in him after that one date, but Carley's always held a grudge."

"I told you all that?"

"We used to talk more," Mom says, with a hurt look in her eyes. I'm guilty of putting it there. I don't say anything back.

The waitress returns and asks what we'd like to eat. Mom orders a plate of onion rings for us to share; I love onion rings. The waitress moves to the next table over, and I watch the father order for his family. I'm aware of my envy as he chats with his daughter and son.

"When did Dad leave?" I ask my mom out of the blue. Her eyes grow wide as she swallows the soda she's just sipped.

"Where did that come from?" she asks. I shrug.

"Is that what's been bothering you lately? You want to know about your dad?"

"Maybe," I say.

Mom fidgets in her seat a little and then clears her throat.

"Okay," she says softly. "I've told you this before and I'll tell you again. Your father and I weren't meant to be together. We didn't get along, and he left when you were six. That's really the end of the story."

I think back to my notes.

"My memory went crazy when I was six. Do you think Dad leaving us traumatized me?"

"I've considered that," Mom admits, looking incredibly uncomfortable.

"So, what, you just fell out of love with each other?" I ask.

My mom doesn't meet my gaze when she replies, "Yes."

"And we never heard from him again?"

"No," she says. The letters at home tell me that she's lying, but I hide my anger. I press the issue.

"He never tried to talk to me or anything?"

I swear I see a flash of guilt in my mother's eyes when she answers. "No, honey, I'm sorry, he never did."

I don't believe you, I think.

And then our onion rings arrive.

When I get home, I try calling Jamie. She picks up on the third ring.

"You need to stop stalking me," she says sharply.

"Hi to you, too," I say.

"Seriously, I got your message earlier. I've gotten all of your messages. When I'm ready to talk to you, I'll call."

"But, Jamie, don't you think we should just talk about it?"

"Do you even remember what it is, London?"

"Yes," I say quietly. My notes are resting on my lap.

"But not really," Jamie snaps at me. "See, you get to go to sleep and forget everything. I don't have that luxury."

"It's not a luxury," I protest.

"Whatever, I have to go now."

"But, J, are we ever going to talk again?"

"I don't know, London, are we?"

Click.

"What's wrong?" Luke asks over the phone.

"Nothing," I lie.

"No, really, what is it? I can hear it in your voice."

I smile weakly. Why can't I remember you?

"Bad day," I reply, shrugging, though he can't see it.

"What happened?" Luke presses. I decide to let him in a little.

"My mom and I aren't really getting along, and she made me go and talk about my *feelings* after school. Then I tried to call Jamie and she basically cut me off and hung up on me. I'm really sick of her drama," I say bitterly, remembering forward to what I would consider some unnecessarily long arguments in the future. "She's just so self-absorbed. Everything is about her. It drives me crazy sometimes!"

Luke laughs a little.

"What?" I reply angrily.

"Nothing, I've just never heard you mad. It's cute."

"It's not cute!" I playfully shout at him. He laughs harder, and I join in. When we stop, Luke asks, "Seriously, though, what can I do to help?"

"It's just nice to talk to you," I say quietly. "This helps."

"I'm sorry I didn't call sooner," Luke says softly, sending chills down my spine. "I was painting."

"It's no big deal," I say, shrugging again. "I was eating onion rings and talking about feelings with my mom anyway."

"So tell me about the..." Luke abruptly stops talking on the other end of the phone. "Just a second," he whispers.

I hear Luke's hand moving over the mouthpiece, and then a woman's muffled voice. Luke's reply is louder but equally jumbled.

Soon enough, he's back.

"Sorry," he says, returning to the conversation. "That was my mom. She wants me to get off the phone. She said it's too late to talk."

"Oh," I say, trying not to sound disappointed, even though I know that my mom would feel the same way. "Okay, I guess we can catch up tomorrow then."

"Okay," Luke says.

"Good night, Luke."

"Sweet dreams, London."

He disconnects the call.

In the darkness, I stare at my phone for a few minutes, reveling in the warm feeling I got from the short conversation with Luke. I know I need to add details of the call to the note on my nightstand, but I don't want to move just yet.

When I've finally willed myself to turn on the light and spoil my Zen moment, my annoying ringtone sounds again, and my heart leaps.

"Hello?" I say quickly.

"I forgot to tell you that you looked really pretty today," Luke says in a whisper.

In the darkness, I feel my face flush.

"Thank you," I whisper back.

"You're welcome."

For a few seconds, we are quiet. Every muscle in my body is tense, in a good way; it's excruciatingly intimate. I'm lying in my bed, clutching the phone like a lifeline, hearing nothing but Luke's measured inhale and exhale and my own quickening heartbeat.

If he were here right now, I'd kiss him. "Well, I guess I should go. My mom might come back," Luke whispers, breaking the moment.

"Okay," I answer, unable to say more.

"See you tomorrow," he says.

"Okay, bye, Luke."

"Bye, London," he says before hanging up, the sound

of my name from his lips sending chills through me again.

I clutch the phone to my chest and exhale sharply, then sit up and snap on the small lamp at my bedside. I update tonight's note, and, as I'm doing so, my own mom pops her head into my room.

"It's late," she says.

"I know, I'm finishing up," I answer, without looking at her.

"Sleep tight," Mom says.

"Thanks."

"I love you, London," she says.

I sigh deeply and say halfheartedly, "I love you, too." My eyes are still on my paper.

I resume writing, and sometime before I finish chronicling my call with Luke and turn out the light, my mom silently disappears.

23

Across the aisle from me, Jamie's floral shoulder bag is packed and ready. There are five minutes left in class, and she's making no effort to appear like she's still paying attention.

I wonder whether she's trying to get detention again.

The thought makes me sick.

Jamie has successfully ignored me all period, a task made easier by the fact that today wasn't a lab day. No partnering. No practice drills. No joint assignments.

No speaking to each other.

The bell rings, and Jamie stands so quickly, it makes me jump. She turns to face me and plunks something down on my desk.

"Here," she says, then turns and exits the classroom.

In fifteen seconds, the room is empty. Even Ms. Garcia is in her attached office, prepping for next period.

Slowly, I unfold the small piece of ripped notebook paper. There is no note; no nothing. Just a phone number.

I know what it is, though.

Even mad at me, Jamie came through.

Now it's up to me to decide whether or not I want to contact my father.

"Do you think I can be fixed?"

My mom looks at me sharply, surprised. We've been eating dinner, up until this point, in silence.

"Fixed?" she asks. "I wouldn't say that you're broken. You're special."

I roll my eyes at her G-rated look on life.

"Whatever, Mom," I reply curtly.

"What made you think of this?" Mom asks, ignoring my tone.

"Anatomy," I reply. I take a bite of chicken and then continue. "Ms. Harris talked about storing different memories in different parts of the brain. Easy stuff, like knowing your name or riding a bike or math, goes in one place; experience-type memories go in another."

"I wouldn't say math is easy," Mom jokes. It annoys me.

"It is for me," I say sharply. "Maybe your math is stored in the harder part. Anyway, that's not the point."

"Sorry," Mom says. "Go on."

"Obviously that means that only one part of my brain is messed up. Not all of it. So I'm wondering if I can have the messed-up part fixed."

And then I'll know what happened in the past, I think, but don't say. And maybe I'll stop remembering what's going to happen in the future, too.

"I don't think it works that way," Mom says quietly.

"Why do you think that?" I demand.

"Because one of the experts we've seen is a neurologist. Do you know what that is?"

"I'm not dense, Mother."

"London, I've about had enough of your tone. I was just going to say that he had an MRI done on your brain, and nothing looked out of the ordinary. He said that your brain is perfectly healthy. No *parts* are 'messed up.'"

"Whatever," I say defensively. "I'm finished."

I push back from the table, take my plate to the sink, and leave my mom to finish eating alone, which only bugs me every step of the way upstairs.

24

"Okay, I'm ready," I whisper, even though whispering isn't necessary. We are totally alone.

Nearly inaudible music plays from Luke's bedroom stereo, and the late-afternoon sun is on the other side of the house, making the room dim.

"Are you sure you want to do this?" Luke asks. The hairs on my arms stand on end.

"Yes," I answer quickly. Then I add, "I think so."

"There's no rush," he offers. "We can wait."

"No, it has to be today," I say, in a bossier tone than I mean.

Luke laughs and picks up his cell phone.

"Okay, here goes," he says.

He dials the number from the scrap of paper, and I bite the fingernail on my right pointer finger in anticipation. I imagine one ring, then two, then...

Luke's eyes widen and his posture stiffens. Less than one second later, he relaxes again. He makes a face as he disconnects the call.

"Wrong number," he says, disappointed.

"Like the voice mail was for someone else?" I ask, needing clarification.

"No, like the number was disconnected. It might have been your dad's number way back when your parents divorced, but he's changed it since then."

As if on cue, muffled squeals erupt from the direction of the kitchen, and Luke and I instinctively move to sit in beanbags. We know — him from experience and me from my notes — that his mother will come in without knocking to see what we're up to. Innocently crank-calling my estranged father might look questionable if we're doing it from Luke's bed.

In fact, anything done while lying on Luke's bed might be met with a raised eyebrow from Mrs. Henry, and a motherly inquisition is not what I need right now.

Luke clicks on the TV just in time for the interruption, and his mom finds us enjoying a documentary about ice fishing. She invites us to the kitchen for an afternoon snack, and we oblige because there's nothing left to do on the dad front for now.

After nachos, we settle into the oversized living room

couch to be entertained by two matching almost-three-year-olds. I know I've spent time with them before, so I try to hide my utter amazement at the carbon copies before me. How odd it must be to see yourself in someone else.

Luke's miniature sisters layer on every piece of dress-up clothing their little bodies will hold and act out a play about "monkeys and mommies at the zoo." We give them a standing ovation, and then explain to them what a standing ovation is.

Next up is a game of skill called "line up the stuffed animals." Like little ants, the girls move from storage bin to line and back again, carrying armfuls of stuffed bears, elephants, giraffes, and more. Once completed, a Great Wall of "Stuffies" extends from the fireplace to the arched doorway. After consulting each other for all of five seconds, they divide the territories: the left half of the living room, which includes the couch, is for "bigs," while the right half is strictly for "princesses."

When Big Luke leaps off the couch and jumps into twin zone, he's met with screams and giggles and general joyousness that's contagious. I can't help but join in for a while, tickling and laughing with either Ella or Madelyn, I can't be sure.

Soon enough, it's nearing dinnertime, and Luke's father arrives wielding a massive box and a warm hello for all of us. Mr. Henry is a handsome man, and I can see Luke in him. For a moment, I let my mind wander, wondering whether Luke will have the same salt-and-pepper hair and lightly weathered face when he's his father's age.

Back in reality, the girls are opening the box with their father's help, and I can't help but feel a pang of jealousy at their relationship. I move to the couch and watch the simple moments that kids with fathers in their lives take for granted. One twin's tiny hand rests on her daddy's shoulder as he cuts open the top; another doll face lights up like it's Christmas morning as her father makes his way through packing peanuts and bubble wrap.

At its core, the box holds a handmade wooden rocking horse, painted pink and ready for riding.

But after one ride each, the real appeal is the massive, fortlike shipping box.

"It's a car!" the twin I think is Ella shouts right into Luke's face. Her eyes are so bright, how could he not help her inside and *vroom* her around the carpeted room? The girl that has to be Madelyn wants a ride, and Ella wants another. And now it's: "My car!" "No, my car!" "No, MINE!"

Clearly adept at solving minibattles, Mr. Henry disappears and then emerges again with a box cutter, some packing tape, and a handful of markers. Ten minutes later, there are two equally wonderful cars, each ready to transport its twin to "the mall," "Grandma's," or "school," as she wishes.

Ella sits tall and holds tight to the sides, surveying the scenery in her imagination. Madelyn opts to lounge back in the car, making it more like a moving bed, which enables her to stare at the ceiling. As Luke scoots her by my feet, I giggle at her serene expression, and wonder what she could be thinking about while lying there staring up at the sky.

And then something happens. A piece snaps into place.

Luke stops his parade float and turns to face me.

"You okay?" he asks quietly.

"Yes," I say quickly. "Why?"

"You just jumped, like something scared you."

"Go, GO!" Madelyn commands from inside the box, when she realizes that her chariot has stopped.

"Shhh," Luke says gently to his sister. "Just a minute." She does as he says, and Luke eases off the floor. He sits down next to me on the couch and takes my hand.

"Are you feeling all right?" he asks softly. "You look really pale." He brushes a stray piece of hair out of my face, and I think I catch Mr. Henry grinning at us.

"I feel sick," I say, louder than I mean to, grabbing the attention of two parents and twin toddlers. Now the whole Henry family is eyeing me, with varying degrees of curiosity and concern.

"Do you want to lie down, London?" Mrs. Henry says, in a way that makes me want to check my reflection. I can't look that bad.

"No, I'm okay," I reply. "I think I just need to go home."

Luke stands, and the twins protest in unison. Mrs.

Henry quiets the girls, while Mr. Henry walks us to the door. Outside, I take a deep breath of freezing air, and, though it burns my lungs, it helps. Luke holds open the door of the van for me and kisses my cheek before he closes it.

We spend the ride in silence, Luke glancing at me every so often with concern on his face. When we pull into my driveway, he offers to come in.

"Thanks, but I'm fine," I say, wanting nothing more than to run inside.

"Is your mom home at least?" he asks, squinting toward the lighted window in the dining room.

"I'm sure she is," I say, turning and adding, "thanks," before slamming the door without so much as a kiss. I jog up the porch steps before Luke has the chance to get out of the car. Once inside the house, I go straight up to my bedroom, close the door, and get in bed fully clothed. Pulling the covers up to my neck, I squeeze my eyes shut and try to control my erratic breathing. I let my mind go to the damp cemetery; I let myself *feel* that I am there, standing in the midst of a sea of black.

I know from my notes that I've had some version of this funeral memory for a while. It has been building and growing in the depths of my brain, quietly reminding me that sometime, someone will die.

But until tonight, "someone" is all I knew.

Then Luke's baby sister lying sweet and serene in a shipping box lit the fuse, and here I am seeing it plain as day: the smaller than usual hole in the ground before me, open wide and already swallowing a tiny coffin fit for the miniperson surely lying inside.

"Someone" is a child.

As if it couldn't get worse, another thought punches me in the gut and beats me down to the point where I consider I might never get up again.

It's hazy—a long time from now—but I do remember being pregnant.

What if it's my child?

Isolated and terrified by what I remember, I pull the covers up tighter under my chin, because it's all I can think to do.

My mom isn't here; my dad is long gone. The only person in my life right now is a boy I can't remember. And someday in my future, I will bury a child.

It is all too much.

25

On the way to Spanish, I check out the Winter Formal posters peppering the hallways; the event is tomorrow night. I know from notes that Luke is taking me, and after spending the last class period with the boy I've apparently been dating for nearly four months, I'm fine with that.

Tense, but fine.

In Spanish, we have a substitute teacher, and Jamie partners with Amber Valentine for pronunciation drills, leaving me to fend for myself against an angry senior TA named Andi who clearly had other plans for the period. I'm not sure what the prerequisites are for obtaining a teacher's assistant gig, but obviously they don't include being good at the subject you're assisting with; Andi's accent is worse than mine.

She's rolled her eyes at me seventeen times and counting, according to the scratch list on my notepad. My revenge is not telling her about the green food particle wedged between her two front teeth.

After class, I rush to catch up with Jamie.

"Hi," I say, when she realizes that I'm walking next to her toward the lunch hall.

"Hey," she says flatly.

"How are you?" I ask, hoping to start mending fences.

"Fine," she says, in an even flatter tone, if that's possible. This is not the day for reconciliation.

"Listen, Jamie, I just wanted to thank you," I offer.

"For what?" she asks, disinterested and avoiding eye contact. I think she just stepped farther away from me.

"For the number. My dad's," I say.

"Don't mention it," Jamie says as she turns in the opposite direction and leaves me standing still in the middle of the busy hallway.

26

Squeaky-clean, and clothed in a red cocktail dress that shows a little more skin than feels natural today, I tap the tune of "Chopsticks" on the antique table.

"You'll wreck your polish," my mom cautions from across the kitchen, nodding in the direction of my freshly painted nails. She's leaning against the counter, watching me as she sips tea from a steaming mug.

I stop tapping but don't reply.

"Are you nervous about the dance?" Mom asks, making conversation.

I hear the grandfather clock in the living room chime once for the half hour. He'll be here any minute.

"I guess," I say, tossing a curl over my shoulder. In truth, it's not the dance I'm nervous about. It's my life.

Trying to push away the darker thoughts, I focus on the notes before me, spread across the table like the diary of an amnesiac. I used the afternoon to study up on Luke as best I could, cramming more for this date than I will for the SAT later this year. Even still, I could forget something. That thought makes me uneasy; I read on.

My mom and I both jump at the sound of the doorbell.

"Want me to get it?" Mom asks when I stay frozen in my seat.

"Huh? Oh, no, I'll go. I mean, I'm dating him, right?"

"Yep, you are," she says warmly. "And he's a very nice boy. You look beautiful, London. Have fun tonight."

I walk toward the kitchen doorway as if my feet are lead and continue down the small hallway leading to the entryway. I turn right, open the door, and there he is.

There...he...is.

Luke.

Tall but not too tall, trim but not buff, perfect hair, glorious eyes, looking comfortable in his simple black suit, even though I know from the notes that he's more partial to rocker chic.

He's holding a gigantic canvas with a bow wrapped around it.

"Instead of a corsage," he says, offering me a painting

of what appears to be my ear. I can see the shadow of the healed piercing that I'll reopen in college.

Wisps of just the right color hair tucked behind. The tiny pitch at the top.

"It's your elf ear," Luke says, grinning. I can't help but laugh and self-consciously touch the body part in question.

He takes a step closer. "It's my favorite ear," he whispers into my left lobe, sending chills down my spine. He stands back again and regards my ensemble. "You look great," he says without hesitation. "Nice shoes."

"Thanks," I say, grinning with my whole body. Most guys don't notice footwear. "You look nice, too. I expected a band T-shirt under your jacket or something."

"Naw..." Luke says with a laugh, showing off a prominent dimple on his right cheek.

I carefully lean the painting against the foyer wall and grab my coat. Luke offers me his hand, and just as we're ready to leave, my mom makes a perfectly timed appearance to wish us well. I could kiss her for being armed with a digital camera and for forcing us to stop and pose before we take off.

Luke leans over and gets the door for me, and once we're out of my mom's earshot, he bends down and whispers, "The dress is hot."

Shivers run down my spine, and I am thrilled that I get to spend the whole night—well, almost the whole night—with him.

Luke drives to school, and because the dance is in the gym, we park in the teachers' lot. Even though it's allowed tonight, it feels scandalous.

Inside, the disco lights rage and the music is one notch higher than deafening. Scanning the room, I see Carley Lynch surrounded by Alex Morgan and some other cheerleaders, all wearing dresses so low-cut that I'm embarrassed for them.

In the opposite corner, I spot Jamie just as her eyes catch mine. Our gazes hold steady for a moment, and then she looks away. In a lovely black dress, she is standing to the right of a boy I don't recognize.

A second passes before my hurt wanes and I remember that Jamie and I will continue to be friends long after this evening. She might not know it right now, but she doesn't hate me.

I follow her eye line, and my stomach lurches a little when I realize that now she's staring at Mr. Rice, who is chaperoning tonight. I consider that I might actually be sick when he gives her an inviting look no married teacher should ever throw in the direction of a sixteen-year-old girl.

Luke must have noticed, too. "Come on, let's dance," he says, before I can get lost in my thoughts.

We move to the center of the dance floor and are immediately awash in a sea of sparkling stars, courtesy of the disco ball. I drape my wrists over Luke's shoulders, and all at once, the strength of his arms around my waist, combined with the melodic song we're swaying to, makes me fantasize about marrying him.

This could be our song.

I let the smooth lyrics carry me away, and I enjoy the moment and the fantasy until it heads down the road toward children. And then the darkness is there, my mind asking questions I don't want to answer.

Is the dead child mine and Luke's? Is that why I don't remember him? Because what we share together will be too painful?

I pull Luke closer and smash my cheek into his shoulder, squeezing my eyes shut in an effort to make the darkness go away. Somehow he knows to hold tighter, too, and though he doesn't see the tear escape my eye, he rubs my back as if to say: "It'll be okay."

I never want to let go.

Luke and I dance like we're glued to each another for three slow songs, before the DJ speeds things up.

My ears fill with a remixed version of a disco classic that will play at practically every wedding and party I'll attend for the rest of my life. The brave kids dance, while those who are either too cool or too awkward move to the outskirts. I'm not sure which group we're in, but we slowly make our way to the fringe.

"Want some punch?" I ask.

"Shouldn't I be asking you that?" Luke asks back.

I shrug and Luke agrees. "I'm going to say hi to Adam,

but I'll meet you for a roll in the snow," he says, pointing to a group of benches decorated with fake snow.

Laughing and shaking my head, I walk to the punch table and grab two clear plastic cups. I wait my turn, fill them, and move to a snowy bench and sit down.

Gabby Stein, from PE, and her date, Christopher Osborne, are sitting on a bench two over from mine. Both look at me like I smell like dirty socks. Neither knows it yet, but Christopher will be valedictorian when we graduate next year.

Right now, however, despite looking uncannily like Superman, Christopher is nothing but a small, helpless animal that's fallen prey to Gabby's boa-constricting embrace. I can't help but long for the PDA police as I quickly look away and wish like crazy for Luke to hurry up.

"Sorry," Luke says when he finally settles in next to me. "Adam's chatty tonight."

"No problem," I say, handing Luke his punch. He chugs it and sets the cup in the snow next to a bunch of other empty cups littering the faux outdoors.

"Having fun?" he asks. His eyes wander to the make-out session two benches down, and he quickly looks back at me.

"Of course, I always have fun with you," I reply, feeling slightly guilty for my use of the word *always*.

"Dance not your scene, though?" he prods, reading my mind.

I let out my breath and laugh. "Not really, no. I mean, it was fun for a few minutes. The slow dances were nice. But these shoes are killing me and I'm hungry."

He laughs with me, then stands and pulls me up with an easy swoop. "Let's go, then," he says.

"Okay, let me just run to the restroom first," I say.

"All right, I'll wait for you by the doors," he replies, kissing me gently before I make my way to the girls' bathroom closest to the gym.

Inside, there are at least five girls admiring themselves in the massive mirror over the sinks. Without catching any eyes, I find an empty stall and then scoot through satin and tulle to a free sink.

Washing my hands, I feel someone's stare in the mirror.

"I know you never asked him about me," Page Thomas says in her most accusatory voice.

This is why I should never come to social events: I am not social. I'm definitely not going to prom.

"Sorry?" I say, pretending not to have heard. Maybe I can stall her long enough so that I can dry my hands and leave.

"You should be," she says, eyes narrowed, face puckered. She spins around, her white-blonde hair trailing after her, and leaves the bathroom.

I'm finished, and the other girls are now staring at me. So, I'm forced to follow Page.

At the end of the hall, Luke is waiting for me. Brad is there, too, waiting for Page. Luke leans against the wall, looking like a suit model. Brad is staring curiously into the trophy case.

Luke's presence must have registered with Page, because she whips around and sees me behind her. She rolls her eyes at me, turns forward, and quickens her pace. When she reaches Brad, she grabs his hand and pulls him back inside the gym.

I can't be sure, but I think I hear her mutter a particularly unkind word about me as they go.

"Making friends tonight, huh?" Luke says with a sympathetic smile. He is holding my coat open for me.

"Let's go," he says, once I'm wrapped and ready.

He grabs my hand, and we rush through the wind toward his minivan, away from it all. In the bitter darkness, my mind wanders to a question that, according to my notes, I've been hoping to answer: Did I change anything with Page, or is she headed down the path toward embarrassment and heartbreak, courtesy of Brad from math?

Even though she clearly has it out for me, I silently hope that somehow Page's fate will be different from what I saw those months before. However nasty she may be, no one deserves that pain.

27

"You're sure she's not home?" Luke whispers as he eyes the front of my house from the driver's seat of his van.

"Yes, I'm sure," I reply at normal volume. "Why are you whispering?"

"I don't know," Luke whispers. He looks at me and flashes a huge, cheesy grin, turns back to the house, and says, "I feel like she can hear me."

"She's not home!" I yell, to prove the point.

"Where is she?" he asks.

"She's at a movie," I answer flatly.

Suddenly, I'm nervous. Luke and I have been dating for several months. Does he expect something? Do I?

Knowing that I could obsess to death about this, I

decide to go for it and leap out of the van. Before I slam the door behind me, I turn to Luke and ask: "Are you coming or what? I need a grilled cheese."

He laughs and kills the engine, then follows my lead. We're inside the warm entryway in no time, removing our jackets and shoes. I can't help but wonder what would happen if I just kept going, removing my dress. . . .

"She left all the lights on. Are you sure she's not coming back soon?"

"Luke! What are you so afraid of?" I playfully shout at him. He's looking back toward the living room to make sure that my mom isn't there.

"Sorry, I know I'm being crazy. I just doubt your mom would want us here alone together this late at night."

"Okay, first of all, are you from the fifties or something? And second of all, it's not that late. It's only . . ." I glance at the ornate wall clock mounted over the piano in the adjacent room. "It's not even nine o'clock. My curfew is midnight. And, third of all, even if she doesn't want us here alone, she'll never know. She's at a movie!"

"What time will it be over?" Luke asks.

"Ten thirty."

"Fine, I'm leaving before ten thirty."

"Fine," I say, grinning.

"Fine," Luke says gently. He's standing over me now, finally calm, rolling up the sleeves of his untucked white dress shirt. The look of him makes my breath catch.

I take a step forward so our faces are just inches away.

Before I think too much about what I'm doing, I stretch up on tiptoe, take Luke's face in my hands, and plant a firm kiss on his soft lips. He doesn't pull away; instead, he bends down slightly, low enough that I don't have to stay on my toes. He wraps his arms tightly around my waist, and I feel his strong palms press into my lower back. My hands move to the back of his neck. I lose track of time and place and just let go and enjoy the increasingly heated kisses.

My heart races, and the thought of shedding clothing comes to mind again. I lean into Luke, and, lip-locked, the two of us stumble backward, until his back thuds into the closed front door. I smash against his chest and it feels like warm marble. He moves his hands into my hair and I breathe heavier as I keep kissing, kissing, kissing him.

The five phones connected to the landline scream in unison and scare Luke and me apart as if we've been caught by some chastity alarm. Realizing the source, and feeling silly both for being startled and for the hormone surge, I nervously laugh, and he joins in.

I take two steps backward, trip over my shoes, and fall to the floor, which sends me into hysterics. Unable to breathe, I roll into a ball of embarrassment, and Luke joins me on the floor, sitting at first, then lying and staring at the ceiling.

The phones finally stop ringing. I manage to compose myself.

"I love your laugh," he says once I've calmed down.

"Thanks, I love to laugh," I reply.

"I know. That's one of my favorite things about you. Remember how spastic you were on our first date? It was cute."

Good to know, I think to myself.

"Tell me more," I say, as perfectly comfortable on the Persian rug as I'd be lying on a couch or a bed. We are head to head, with our bodies at angles: if someone observed us from overhead, they'd see a V.

"Mmmm, you want to know the reasons why I love you?" he asks casually, as if he's said those words to me before. But if I'm remembering my notes correctly, this is the first time.

My heart is threatening to break free from my chest, but I present a calm exterior. "Yes, a list, if you will."

He lets out a quiet chuckle.

"There are too many reasons to have a complete list, but I'll name a few."

"Please, go on," I say, attempting to remain steady when I feel like bouncing. I hold my breath.

"Well, there's the obvious. You're beautiful."

"Yes, obviously," I reply flatly, masking the fact that my stomach just did cartwheels.

"I love your hair. This sounds crazy, but when I first saw you in that ridiculous outfit with your long red hair flying out all over the place, I just wanted to touch it. It's soft, and it always smells good. In fact, hold on...." Luke leans over and buries his nose in my hair. He takes a deep breath, then returns to his back.

"Ah, the best," he mutters.

"You are a total weirdo," I joke. He ignores me.

"Let's see...what else? I love you because you're the type of person to befriend a new guy on his first day of school. Oh, and speaking of friends, I love that you haven't given up on Jamie, even though she's mad at you and not being very cool."

"She's worth it," I say in her defense.

"Yeah, that's what I mean. You're not into cliques and all that crap. You're mature."

"Right. What did you say about laughing fits?"

"Well, yes, there are those. Most of the time, you're mature." Luke pokes me in the ribs and grins before facing the ceiling once again.

"What else?" I prompt him. "This is fun!"

"Let's see," Luke says, folding his left forearm behind his head. He looks to the wall where his painting leans. "I like that you don't think it's strange that I like to paint ears."

"I do, a little. But I like strange," I say. "What else?"

"I don't know, London," he says, rolling to his side to face me and propping his head on his hand. "I think it's just the whole package. I can't pick you apart. I just love all of you. I think I always have."

I wonder what he means by "always" as he brushes my face with his hand and we are quiet for a moment. It doesn't sit quite right, but, not wanting to ruin the moment, I say, "I love all of you, too."

The words are weighty, but I mean them, and I think Luke does, too. And, strangely, for their heaviness, I feel light. This feels easy.

We lie here, Luke and I, inhaling each other's breath and listening to the ticktock of the clock, when a very unpleasant gurgling growl erupts from the depths of me.

"Was that your stomach?" Luke asks, looking down at my abdomen.

"Yes!" I blurt out, before launching into a fresh wave of delirium. "I...told...you...I...was...hungry!" I manage to say between gasps for breath. He shakes his head at me and then slowly stands up. The sight of him towering above me in all his gorgeousness steals my giggles.

"Let's get you a grilled cheese," he says, offering me his hands.

"Finally!" I say back, allowing him to pull me from the floor. Once I'm standing, I shiver: the cold from the tile beneath the rug made it through me.

"Cold?" he asks.

"Yep. I'm going to go grab a sweatshirt. You make yourself comfortable in the kitchen."

I run up the stairs and search my bedroom for something fuzzy and warm. Nothing in plain view, I hit the closet light and start pulling folded items from the shelf. I evaluate my options and settle on a tan hoodie that I know from my notes is Luke's.

Checking my reflection in the mirror, I decide to take the extra minute to pull my hair back into a ponytail. As I wrap the hair tie once, twice, then three times, my eyes scan the room, seeing it as Luke might.

If I let him come up here tonight.

The bed is beautifully made: Mom must have tidied up after we left for the dance. The throw pillows are lined up just so.

There is a photo of Luke and me in a dark wooden frame on the desk. I don't remember when it was taken.

In the corner, the hamper is empty.

On the nightstand are the lamp and an empty coaster where a used tea mug sat earlier. My mom really must have cleaned. . . .

Wait.

For a blink, I look back to the nightstand in the mirror. Then I turn around on the stool to see it firsthand.

It looks so . . . bare.

Because it is.

Because it is!

My pulse quickens as I quiz myself.

Where are my notes?

Did Mom move them? Did she put them away?

No, she wouldn't do that. Or would she? I stand and rush across the room. I check the nightstand drawer and the desk drawers, too.

I chew my pointer fingernail, thinking. I turn slowly around the room, scanning every surface.

Did I take them somewhere?

Where would I take them?

Where did I have them last?

My breath sucks in almost before I fully realize what's happened.

I know where my notes are.

They're right where I left them.

Right where I was reading them before Luke picked me up tonight.

Right where I sent Luke to hang out.

They're in the kitchen.

"Luke!" I shout, running out of my bedroom and down the stairs, as if it will make any difference. "Luke!" I shout again in vain.

I know even before I'm down the stairs that he's already seen them.

No answer comes from the direction of the kitchen. I quicken my pace and nearly slip on the polished hardwood while rounding the corner to the kitchen.

"Luke," I say again, to his back. He faces the table and doesn't speak.

"Luke?" I try a gazillionth time.

He turns, holding a single letter in his hands.

I stand, frozen, staring at him.

Finally, he speaks.

"I wondered how you did it," he says.

Still frozen, I'm confused.

"Did what?" I ask.

"How you remembered me this time," he says. "I mean, I've caught you a few times, forgetting things. But most of the time, you seem . . . normal. You seem to recognize me each day."

My furrowed eyebrows rise as my eyes widen with the shocking confirmation that he knows.

Luke knows. For a moment, it's almost a relief. I don't have to work so hard. I don't have to . . .

Wait, Luke knows?

Then, I realize. For four months now, the boy before me has been lying to me.

He's as bad as my mother.

Is there anyone in my life who isn't deceiving me?

The relief is gone; the anger is here. My shoulders fall and my arms draw close, as if to protect myself from the world. Blood rushes to my face and my ears pound. My heart races.

I find it difficult to speak. But finally I'm able.

"You knew?" I ask, boiling.

"Yes, London, I knew," he says, smiling hesitantly, as if he doesn't know whether he should.

The smile sends me over the edge. My hands tighten into fists, and I feel the urge to scream at the top of my lungs.

"For how long?" I hiss, putting a hand on the counter to steady myself. I think of the cards from my father. The betrayal from my mother. And now this.

"Since we were eleven," Luke says matter-of-factly, fueling the fire that's already raging in my veins.

"Luke, what the hell are you talking about?" I shout. I

stare at him, feeling wronged. I want him to leave. But I want him to explain first.

"Okay," he begins. "Do you remember..." He sweeps his hand over the pile of papers. "Do you remember me mentioning that I spent a few summers with my aunt and uncle?"

Glad that I took the time to study my notes today, I mutter, "Yes."

"And do you also remember that you went to day camp at the YMCA when you were younger?"

"No."

"Well, you did. And so did I. My aunt and uncle live here, London. Or at least my aunt does. They're going through a divorce. One of the reasons we moved here was so my mom could be closer to her sister."

I exhale loudly. I'm still gripping the counter with one hand; the fingernails on the other are about to draw blood from my palm. Jaw clenched, I imagine myself biting through my own molars. Luke reads my body language and gets the hint.

"All that's beside the point," he says. "The point is that we went to the same camp for a summer. We were friends. You were my only friend. And I'm pretty sure I was your only friend back then, too."

Luke pauses to make sure that the information is settling in. I stare sharply at him, and he takes my silence as a cue to go on.

"None of the other kids gave me the time of day,

because I didn't live here. And of course, there was the dodgeball incident."

I raise my eyebrows slightly without speaking a word. I am livid, but also curious.

Luke shrugs like it was no big deal. "We were all playing dodgeball and one of the bigger kids purposely hurled the ball at my face when the counselor wasn't looking. My nose broke, but I have a high tolerance for pain, so I picked a fight with the kid and smiled as he pummeled me. I thought it would make me look cool. Instead, everyone thought I was a freak. Everyone except you."

I roll my eyes at the compliment. I'm not giving in that easily.

"I noticed you the first day of camp. I watched you reading alone in the corner, keeping to yourself. I wanted to talk to you but I was chicken. And I seriously wanted to touch your hair back then, too. I wasn't kidding about that earlier."

Remembering our conversation on the rug, I experience a different kind of heat for an instant. Then I remember that, just like my mother, my boyfriend is a liar.

I cross my arms over my chest, and Luke anxiously clears his throat. I think he knows he's about to get kicked out, so he races through the rest of the story.

"Anyway, you came up to me after the fight and helped me. You gave me your sweater to stop the bleeding. It was totally ruined. I thought it was poetic or something to give you my sweatshirt that day outside the gym," he says as an aside, gesturing to the hoodie I'm wearing. "But of course, you didn't get that," he adds.

"I can't help it!" I shout.

"I know," Luke says. "I didn't mean it like that." He shifts and I check the clock. I hope with all my might that my mother doesn't come home and interrupt our conversation.

"It's almost ten," Luke says.

"I can tell time," I fire back at him.

"Do you want me to leave?"

"Yes," I say harshly. "But finish first."

"Okay, well, anyway, at camp, the day after the fight, I came up to you and said hello, and you didn't remember who I was. At first, I was hurt. I thought you were pretending not to know me. Like you were too cool or something. But you were nice, and chatty. So, I thought you had amnesia or something. I asked you if there was something wrong with your brain. You said, 'No, is there something wrong with yours?'"

One corner of Luke's mouth turns up a little as he remembers the exchange. He waits a beat, and then continues.

"Anyway, I kept asking in different ways, and finally you pulled me to a corner and told me that you had a big secret. That you remembered the future but not the past. You made me swear not to tell anyone, and I never did."

Luke pauses, and I stare at him silently. Realizing he's not getting props for secret keeping, he goes on.

"So, every day, we'd meet each other again. We had a lot of the same conversations over and over. But we had a lot of new ones, too. Sometimes we'd sit in the bottom of one of those climbing things that looked like Swiss cheese, and try to figure out who the kids were by the shoes they had on. It was really fun. You were good at that game."

I am taken aback by the realization that the "foot game" I'll play forever came from my childhood relationship with Luke. I'm curious about that, but I hold back. Anger is easier right now.

Luke's smiling wistfully, which makes me even madder. I roll my eyes and let out my breath, and he gets it. Nostalgia wiped clean from his face, he goes on. "When I moved here I thought maybe you'd remember me. But then, especially that night we fell asleep in the van...I knew for sure."

There is a little tug on my heart when I hear the sadness in his voice. But I hold my ground.

"Is that it?"

"London, I'm really sorry for not telling you sooner," he says, taking two slow steps toward me, like he's approaching a wild animal.

Instinctively, I edge backward, away from the guy I couldn't get close enough to minutes ago.

"You mean you're sorry for lying," I say harshly. "For betraying me. For taking advantage of my situation."

"That's a little extreme," Luke says with a small laugh.

"I mean, you've pretty much been lying to me, if you think about it." He almost smirks now, which sends me into a tailspin.

"It's not the same!" I shout at him. "You have no idea how it feels to completely forget every single day. I wake up not knowing what I wore to school the day before, let alone what stupid things I may have said or done. I remember things that no one—*no one*—should have to anticipate experiencing. Horrible things. Things that are going to happen to me..."

Tears are streaming down my face now. Luke takes another step toward me and I put up a hand to stop him. I keep ranting through the sobs.

"I've got enough going on, and now this. My best friend has gone off the deep end. My mom is lying to me, and apparently you've been lying, too."

Something hits me and I interrupt myself.

"Wait, if I knew you, why didn't my mom tell me that when she met you again? Or was that just another one of her lies? Were you in this together?"

Luke looks down and away. His cheeks flush.

"I never met her in person, and she wouldn't know my name because I went by something else back then."

"What?" I ask, curious despite my anger.

"L.J." Luke says sheepishly. "I thought I was tough, and that all tough guys went by their initials." He takes another step.

"Stop," I command, finding no amusement in Luke's

childish confession. "Whatever your name is or was, the point is that you lied. You could have pieced together some of my past for me. You could have actually helped me, Luke. Can't you see that? But you didn't. You willingly deceived me. I can't believe you'd do that to me. To someone you supposedly love. To someone who *thought* she loved you."

Luke's face falls and he's silent for a few seconds. Then he brushes away two tears that escape his blue eyes. He looks helpless, and part of me wants to hug him.

Instead, when I can control myself enough to speak again, I say, almost choking, "Just go."

"London, I'm so sorry. I didn't think it would upset you this much. I wasn't trying to . . ." His voice fades and his head hangs for a moment. Then he looks up at me and our eyes hold steady. "I just didn't want you to have to feel self-conscious around me."

I shake my head and back out of the kitchen doorway so that he can leave. His shoulders are slumped as he walks by me on the way to the foyer.

From the kitchen, I hear him put on his shoes and then open and quietly close the front door behind him. I hear the van start and rev; when its gentle hum fades into the night, I crumble to the kitchen floor.

Despite it being after midnight, my hushed ringtone sounds from beneath the pillow for the third time in an hour. There are voice mails waiting to be deleted once

I can touch my phone without accidentally answering his call.

It's amazing how much stuff one can accumulate after dating someone only four months. A mini-mountain of notes and photos are piled high in the fancy hatbox from my closet. The hatbox is meant for mementos. Instead, it will be a time capsule never intended to see the light of day.

Girls the world over will be envious of my ability to dole out the perfect heaping of revenge to the boy who wronged me. Done crying now, I summon the ability that I and I alone seem to possess, and channel what surely would be Jamie's sound advice were she here to give it.

"Forget him," she'd say.

"Good plan," I say aloud.

Sweeping away the sweetness and focusing on the bad, I smash the hatbox pile to make room for the last few items. Before closing the lid, I add the note scratched in barely dry ink, explaining what he did to deserve this fate should I uncover the box in the future.

The note for my mom is on the kitchen table: the one that summarizes the breakup and instructs her never to speak of Luke again.

The job is almost complete.

I delete the voice mails without listening to them and erase his number from my cell. When I'm positive that my mom is out cold, I sneak to the basement to hide my failed relationship among old kitchen appliances, boxes of notes from years gone by, and worn toys littering the junk closet beneath the stairs.

I don't linger to consider the ramifications of erasing Luke from my thoughts. Instead, I switch off the basement lights, hurry back up the stairs, and scoot deep beneath the covers. I think of Luke until I fall asleep.

Sleep comes too quickly tonight.

28

A hand grips my left elbow just as I'm getting ready to retrieve my Anatomy book from the depths of my locker. The note said I didn't finish my homework this weekend, so I need to do it in study hall.

I wince at the elbow grip, not because it's rough but because my arm still hurts from when I managed to fall on it during first-period PE, playing volleyball, of all things. You don't even move that much in volleyball, yet I dislodged a tiny piece of elbow bone. At least that's what it feels like. It's probably just another bruise.

"Ouch," I say, spinning to face the grabber. I don't know who I was expecting, but surely it wasn't him.

The gorgeous boy drops his grip on my arm and recoils like he's been burned. In his perfect blue eyes, I see confusion, anger, hurt, and even a touch of pleading. I don't recognize him, but I wish I did.

"I didn't mean to hurt you," he says softly. His voice is smooth and oddly relaxing.

"Oh, no, it's not your fault," I say, rubbing my elbow. "I fell on it in gym class. I'm a bit of a klutz."

The boy smiles a sad smile then, and a hint of a dimple appears on his right cheek. My stomach flips over, and suddenly I'm very aware of myself. I shift awkwardly from one foot to the other.

Realizing that I'm staring, I break my gaze and turn back to my locker to get the book I was after in the first place.

"Can I help you with something?" I ask, still facing the locker in an effort to appear nonchalant.

"I need to talk to you," the boy says quietly.

I stuff the book, a notepad, and a spare pen from the top shelf into the oversized gray and white striped shoulder bag I found in the hall closet this morning, and slam the locker door shut. The hall is crowded now, and the girl with the locker next to mine exhales loudly as she tries to get to her own belongings. The boy is blocking her way.

"Oh, sorry," he says to her when he realizes his blunder.

"Whatever." She shoves her way past him.

The boy has moved to block my way now, and I begin

to rethink my desire to remember him. There's a slightly creepy sense of urgency about him.

"Are you okay?" I ask, wondering whether there's something wrong with him. Is this kid going to freak out on me? Is that why I don't remember him?

Gripping my bag like a security blanket, I take a step to the right to try to move around him, but he anticipates my move and blocks me again. He bends slightly and looks directly into my eyes before speaking.

"No, London, I'm not okay. We have one fight and that's it? You won't return my calls. You weren't home yesterday when I came by. We need to talk about this."

When he finishes, he straightens slightly but doesn't stop with the eye contact. I don't know what to do, so I opt for honesty.

"I'm really sorry, but I have no idea what you're talking about. I don't even know you." I smile weakly as if to console a friend.

It's like a lightbulb turns on in the boy's head. He stands completely straight and his eyes narrow. He shakes his head and then looks at me with even more venom.

"Real mature, London. Thanks a lot," the boy hisses. He turns and strides down the main hall in the direction I need to go.

The girl with the locker next to mine giggles as she passes; she's heard the whole conversation. "I'll take him if you don't want him."

I wait until there's no sign of the boy before I weave

my way to study hall. As I move, I review what happened and end up just as confused. I open the massive library doors and walk through the metal detectors, happy to have one whole class period to ponder the situation.

And, oh yeah, do my Anatomy homework.

But then, as I approach the bank of tables reserved for study hall, I realize my bad fortune.

The brooding boy sits alone at the only table with any free seats.

Of course he does.

Surprisingly, the gorgeous freak is otherwise engaged all period long, so I manage to finish my homework with time to spare. Even so, I can't help but notice the huffs and snorts coming from the boy as he writes furiously in his notebook. Angry much?

Now, as I sit packed and ready to leave the moment the bell rings in forty-four... forty-three... forty-two seconds, the boy is still writing. I can't help but watch the muscles on his toned left forearm flex as he moves the pen across the page. His worn T-shirt looks baby-soft and hangs perfectly across his shoulders and chest. I find myself wanting to touch the waved lock of hair that peeks out from behind his right ear....

"What?" the boy snaps as he looks right at me. Several other clock-watching students turn in our direction.

"Nothing," I whisper, looking back to the industrial wall-mounted clock that tells me I'll be free from this

uncomfortable situation in twenty...nineteen...eigh-
teen...seconds.

I hear the boy rip the pages he's been working on from
his notebook, which strikes me as odd, since I'd think
he'd want to keep them safe until class.

Finally, the bell rings, and I stand so quickly to leave
that I practically knock my chair back.

"Wait," he says in a softer tone. Instead of running, I
turn to face him.

"Please read this," he says, offering me what I realize
now is a letter. It's folded in half, with my name written
on the outside.

"Okay," I say as he brushes past me, leaving me confused and alone in a barren library with a warm and oddly
familiar scent lingering behind him.

I skip the trip to my locker before math, opting instead
to arrive early and see what on earth this boy could be so
mad at me about.

Minutes later, I realize that being early was a good
choice.

Dear London,
    First off, let me just say that I love you.
Keep that in mind as you read on....
    My name is Luke Henry and I've been
your boyfriend since I started at Meridan
in October. You don't remember me in your

future for some reason we haven't sorted out yet, but I'd like the chance to find out why.

You're really mad at me right now, and rightly so. I never told you that we'd met, but we had. When we were younger, we went to camp together. I was fascinated by you and how, every day, you'd befriend me again even though you didn't remember me from the day before. You were my first real crush, and now you're my first real love.

After the Winter Formal on Saturday night, I found the notes that you used to remember me and I told you the truth. You were right when you said that I'd been lying to you for all this time. I'm so sorry, London, and all I want is the chance to redeem myself. I have no idea why I did it. Maybe I thought you'd think I was a stalker. Maybe I just wanted to see if you'd ever wake up and know who I was.

You didn't.

But, London, we're good together. I don't want to lose you. I made a huge mistake, but I hope that you can consider forgiving me. Because like I said in the beginning, I love you, London Lane.

Always.

Luke

*   *   *

After school, a floral hatbox sits before me with its innards exposed. Luke's apology letter in one hand and a photo of a happy couple in the other, I feel like my innards are exposed, too.

My mom didn't seem surprised when I asked her about him. She led me right to the hatbox, with a look that bordered on patronizing.

"Well, that didn't take long," she said.

"It's not over yet," I replied, grabbing the hatbox and taking refuge in my room.

Now, in a word, I'm thrown.

I started at the beginning, and after reading about the first few times Luke and I spoke, I was ready to dial his number and accept his apology right then and there.

But then I read on, with his betrayal in mind. Every seemingly pleasant moment filtered through this new lens of lies became darker—dirtier. He was keeping a secret from me the whole time, never letting me know the real Luke.

Then again, I was keeping a secret from him, too.

In a way, we were both at fault.

Still, his lie was worse.

Wasn't it?

My cell phone rings beside me and I know that it's him, even though the number isn't stored in my phone. I consider ignoring the call, but can't help but answer.

"Hello?" I say quietly.

"Hi." A smooth voice breathes into the phone, sending

chills down my spine. Why did he lie? If I wasn't mad at him, I could be staring into his blue eyes right now.

"Hi," I say back.

"I know you said that you needed time, but I had to call," Luke begins.

"You're not exactly giving me space," I say, determined not to be charmed so easily. Gorgeous or not, he hurt me.

"I know," he says softly, sounding helpless. "What can I do?"

"You can't do anything," I say firmly. "I said I needed space to figure this out, and if you really care about me, you'll respect that."

I wince and think he might have, too, although I can't be sure. He's silent for a few seconds.

"Okay, London," he says finally, with a sadness that breaks my heart a little. "I'll leave you alone."

Instead of telling him "never mind," like I desperately want to, I simply say, "Thank you, Luke," and disconnect before I make any promises I might not be able to keep.

Leaning against my bed with the gutted hatbox before me and chronicles of our relationship littering the floor, I can't help but cry. I don't want to be sensible. I don't want to think about things. I don't want to have to forgive him.

I don't want him to have lied in the first place.

I shove the debris off my legs and climb up onto my bed, lying facedown in my pillow and sobbing for who knows how long. I don't hear her come in but my mom appears, smoothing my hair and patting my back and telling me it'll all be okay.

No, it won't, I think to myself.

It won't be okay at all.

29

Life blindsided me this morning.

It's barely past seven o'clock on a Wednesday, and already I'm tired. It seems everything is wrong, so I focus on something small.

Page Thomas.

Yesterday's note says that she served as a captain in gym class. When I was the last person on the bench, Page told Ms. Martinez and the class that she'd rather play one person short than have me on her team.

Nice.

I moved on to reading about Luke, but then something in a note from four months ago caught my attention. It was around the time Luke moved to town:

Bring yoga pants, T-shirt for gym (had to borrow clothes from Page Fri.)

Yesterday, Page wouldn't have lent me a square of toilet paper, let alone a shirt. I remember her tomorrow and there's no way she'd lend me anything then, either. Curious, I spend the next hour searching through notes for entries about her. And what I realize is this:

I saved Page Thomas.

Okay, sure, it wasn't from a forty-story building sent up in flames or anything. But, looking back now, I see clearly there was a time when I remembered Brad breaking Page's heart. Demolishing it, actually.

But this morning, when I think of Page and Brad, I remember them together until I can't remember them at all. I'll hear at the senior party that they're going to college together; that's the last they'll be in my life.

As far as I can tell from notes, things changed when I lied about Brad not liking girls. Page was forced to find another way into Brad's arms, and it seems to have made all the difference.

So, yes, I am friendless. And, yes, I've been wronged by an apparently gorgeous and wonderful guy. I'm living with a mom I can't trust and dreading the worst kind of heartbreak imaginable in the form of a dead child.

My life is screwed up, to say the least.

But the tiny smidgen of a tidbit of a crumb of a shaving of sunshine on this bleak Wednesday morning is that I saved Page Thomas from heartbreak. With one simple decision months ago, I changed something for the better.

And if I can help her, surely I can help myself.

I have the metal door positioned in a way that allows me to keep watch on Jamie Connor's locker across the hall without being obvious about it. I'm staring into the magnetic vanity mirror, waiting. Of course, I look like I'm in love with myself, but no one is paying attention to me anyway.

Because I can see what's behind me, I know that the boy I'm assuming is Luke, thanks to photos in my bedroom this morning, walked by earlier, slowly, hesitantly, like he wanted to stop.

But he didn't.

He's waiting; that's good.

Finally, a familiar blunt blonde haircut catches my eye, and I turn to confirm that Jamie has arrived. She's in too-tight faded jeans and a hot-pink top that seems innocent enough from the back but which I know, without having to look, is low-cut in the front.

I slam the metal door so that the lock catches securely and ease my way across two lanes of students, eyes on

Jamie's back the whole time. Once I reach her, I have to clear my throat before she notices me standing at her side.

"Hi, J," I say brightly.

"Hi," she mutters, turning back to her locker.

"How are you?" I ask.

"Do you care?" she says, not turning around.

"Of course I care, Jamie, you're my best friend!" She glances at me, then back to the locker.

"Am I?" she says. "Or am I too much of a slut to be your friend anymore?"

"Jamie, that's not fair!" I say. Jamie slams her locker door and turns to face me. Her eyes are cold, vacant.

"No, London. No, it isn't," she says bitterly, before walking off toward her first class.

My face flushes, and I'm so mad that I want to chase after her and shake her and tell her everything I know that she doesn't. But just then, the bell signaling the start of the period rings, and chasing down Jamie might mean detention with her boyfriend, I mean Mr. Rice. So instead, I rush to the library.

Ms. Mason glares at me for being late, and Luke sits up expectantly when I fall into the chair opposite him, but something about my body language tells them both to back off. I work on Spanish homework the whole period and leave quickly when the bell sounds. I can feel Luke's disappointment, and guilt creeps through me until I remember this morning's notes. This is the guy who lied to me for four months. Four months. He deserves a little indecision. He deserves to sweat it out a bit.

Skipping the trip to my locker, I settle into my seat in Spanish and watch the door. I'm ready to confront Jamie before class, but the seconds tick by and her desk remains empty. The bell rings, and there's no Jamie.

Ten minutes later, she's still not here.

When I've decided that she's ditched class, gone home sick, or left for a doctor's appointment, I face the fact that there will be no confrontation today. Jamie had the last word, and it was a nasty one. My anger subsides because it has to, and it's replaced by sadness. I can't help but feel that my best friend has abandoned me.

And I get it, at least a little. I know she's upset. I know she's jealous of Luke. I know she wishes I didn't disapprove of her boyfriend, if you want to call Mr. Rice that.

But getting it doesn't make it stop hurting.

Forever, I will share my thoughts and feelings with Jamie. Forever, except for right now. And right now, I really need her.

She should be here to exchange notes about whether or not to forgive Luke. She should be here to whisper with me about my dad. She should calm me—just by being nearby—about things too awful to know. She should willingly partner with me for stupid pronunciation drills.

But I'm alone, not just for pronunciation drills. For

everything. Every morning when I wake up and learn this anew, a fresh wound will open—until the day Jamie decides to forgive me.

And then we'll be fine again.

Because that's how I remember it.

30

The house line rings twice before my mom answers it. I can hear her muffled voice from the kitchen below my bedroom. A minute later, there's a quick knock on the door.

"London, are you up?" she whispers through the door.

"Yeah, Mom, I'm awake. Come on in," I say from my seat at the desk. I'm surprised she didn't hear me moving around earlier. I've been up for hours.

"There's a woman on the phone for you," she says.

"Weird," I say before pushing back in my desk chair and walking to the telephone table in the hallway. I pick up the receiver and wait until my mom makes her way down to the kitchen and hangs up the other extension.

"Hello?"

"London?"

"Yes, this is London. Who's this?" I say, twirling the phone cord around my index finger.

"This is Abby Brennan. We met a few months ago?"

My mind is blank. I'm silent.

"You came to my house? You were looking for your grandmother, Jo Lane?"

"Oh, yes," I lie into the phone. I have no clue. This was not in my notes. "How are you?"

"I'm fine, thank you," the woman says kindly. I can hear a child's voice in the background, singing a song about snakes on parade. "Chelsea, Mommy's on the phone, honey. Sorry about that, London."

I can't hear the little girl's response, but I don't hear the snake song anymore, either.

"No problem."

"Anyway, I'm calling because I remembered the name of your grandmother's retirement home in the city. It's been driving me crazy for months, and finally this week it came to me."

My stomach tightens into knots. I've been reading notes all morning; how did I miss this?

"Oh, really?" I say to the woman, hoping to sound casual.

"Yes, it's called Lingering Pines."

"That's great," I say robotically, even as my mind spins out of control.

"Yes, well, I just wanted to let you know. When you speak to her, please tell Jo that the house is being well taken care of. Give her our best."

"I will," I say mindlessly before telling the woman good-bye and hanging up the phone.

In the remaining forty-five minutes before school, I carefully dress, apply makeup, and flat-iron my hair, all the while pondering what just happened.

Somehow, I clearly managed to figure out that my grandmother's name is Jo Lane. Then, apparently I went to Abby Brennan's house looking for said grandmother. And now, I guess that my grandmother, Jo Lane, is in a nursing home.

Called Lingering Pines.

In the city.

What I don't get is, why? Why wouldn't I chronicle all of this for myself?

All I can fathom as I apply a top layer of lip gloss is that when I researched my grandmother, I felt that I'd come up empty. All I can rationalize is that I didn't want to torture myself with knowing that I failed. All I can figure is that I gave up.

But now I have the name of my grandmother's nursing home. I can contact her, if I want to. And she might lead me to my father.

Looking in the mirror, I smile at my reflection. I feel powerful with this new information, with my stick-straight hair; long, dark lashes; and fitted black button-down.

And feeling powerful is a good thing, because apparently there's a boy in my life who needs to be reminded to never, ever wrong me again.

"What are your plans for tonight?" my mom asks hours later at dinner.

"I don't know," I say, avoiding direct eye contact. "Maybe I'll watch a movie."

Really, I can't wait to Google Lingering Pines and call to confirm that my grandmother is a resident. After that, who knows?

"I shouldn't be too late," Mom says. "It's only two houses."

I shrug; she can stay out all night for all I care.

"I bought some popcorn," Mom offers, trying a little too hard.

"Okay, thanks," I say, scooping up the last of my peas and wishing she'd leave already, or at least stop watching me eat. I give her a broad, cheesy (fake) smile that, thankfully, she buys. Mom walks across the room, kisses the top of my head, and grabs her keys.

"I guess I'd better get going, then. Have a good night, sweetie. Let's do something fun tomorrow, just us girls, okay?" She pauses by the door to the garage, waiting.

"Okay, Mom," I say reassuringly so she'll leave. Seconds later, it works.

Hastily, I rinse my plate and put it in the dishwasher before skipping up the stairs and waking up my computer from sleep mode. In less than a minute, not only do I have the number for Lingering Pines, but I'm halfway through the photo gallery of images of its sweeping grounds, happy residents, and well-maintained facilities. Though I assume that the people in the pictures are models, I carefully inspect each photo just in case, then print the main page and some of the photos for reminders.

I have the jitters as I ponder what I'm about to do. Step one: find Grandma. Step two: find Dad.

Before I have the chance to talk myself out of it, I open my cell phone and dial the main number for Lingering Pines. The tone sounds long and lonely. I picture a dated phone waiting unattended, its shrill call going unnoticed over too-loud TVs shouting from the patients' rooms.

I wish for a receptionist to pick up the second before she does. Except that it's a recording telling me that Lingering Pines is closed, and to please call again tomorrow or dial one for the nurse's station.

Apparently the elderly residents of Lingering Pines Retirement Community are only open for business between the hours of 8:00 AM and 5:00 PM daily.

Feeling that this isn't earth-shattering enough to disturb a nurse, I hang up. I store the number in my contacts, allowing myself to imagine for a moment what it would be like to have a grandmother to call and visit sometimes.

Later, long after I've left high school behind, I will envy my friend Margaret's relationship with her grandmother. I will cry when she dies of cancer, not because I'll know her that well but because I'll see Margaret lose a little piece of herself when the sweet old woman goes.

Nothing left to do on my grandmother search this evening, I turn off the computer, wash the day from my face, and head downstairs to make popcorn and watch a movie, just like I told my mom I would.

In the kitchen, I get out the kernels and the mini-kettle. I scan the directions on the popcorn container, then add the oil and kernels to the pan, turn on the stove, and start slowly turning the crank. The first kernel explodes, then the second, then twelve or twenty or fifty more. Concentrating on nothing but the span of time between the tiny explosions so as not to burn my precious popcorn, I barely notice the sound from the front entryway. In fact, by the time I pause to listen, I wonder whether I heard anything at all.

Then it's there again: a timid knock at the front door.

Not the doorbell.

A knock.

Still holding the handle of the popcorn pan, I glance at the clock. It only feels like midnight. Really, it's 6:58, a perfectly appropriate time for accepting visitors on a Friday night. If only I were *expecting* visitors.

Immediately, I wonder if today's outfit worked; I wonder if it's Luke. I find myself hoping that it is, even though I'm still hurt by his actions.

I set the popcorn aside and hurry from the kitchen. I switch on the porch light and wish our door had a peephole.

"Who is it?" I call.

There is a pause, and I consider backing away from the door and calling my mom to come home. Maybe it's not him. Finally:

"It's Luke."

I suck in my breath. Then I wait a beat and open the door.

The waves of Luke's hair are rustling in the winter wind and his cheeks are flushed from the cold. He briefly removes one hand from his jeans pocket to wave hello without speaking the word itself, and then replaces his hand. He looks boyish and a touch embarrassed to be here, shuffling his feet as I open the door wider.

I wrap my arms around my torso to shield myself from the frigid outdoors, but it doesn't really help. I'm freezing, but I don't mind.

Luke is here.

He looks around, and then suddenly his blue eyes are on mine, invading my space and my soul. I feel self-conscious from his piercing stare, but no part of me wants to break free from it, either.

"Is your mom here?" Luke asks, in a tone both soft and strong. Feeling weak, I tighten the grip on my torso for support.

"No, she went . . ."

Before I can finish my sentence, Luke is up the entryway step, kissing me.

Hard.

His palms are on either side of my face, and the few feet that were between us have shrunk to inches. One inch, maybe.

I drop my arms in surrender, then slowly wind them around this boy before me, tight and then tighter still. Luke kicks shut the front door behind him, lips still locked on mine, and we kiss each other like one of us is dying.

"I can't stay away from you," he whispers when he finally takes a break to breathe. He's staring directly into my eyes with his forehead pressed against mine, and his hands are still holding tight to my face, as if to keep me there and ensure that I look at him right back.

To ensure that I see him. And, boy, do I.

His eyes look pained yet determined. I can see in them that he's not letting go, and I know for sure now that I don't want him to, either.

"Don't stay away from me, then," I whisper back, placing my hands gently over his and lowering them to my neck and then my sides. The movement relaxes him a little, and I can tell that his angst is waning.

"Do you forgive me, London?" Luke asks, his eyes still cutting into me.

"Yes, I do," I say truthfully.

Yes, he lied to me. But he loves me, and I love him, and people make mistakes. I can't see him in my future to know for sure, but I believe he'll learn from this. He seems to be that type of person.

Luke is kissing me again now, softer this time. I try to think of nothing and just enjoy the moment, but I can't help but wonder when my mom will return.

The house shifts, and I jump away from Luke like we've been caught.

"What?" he asks, looking around.

"Nothing," I say, peeking behind me just to make sure. "I just thought my mom was back."

"Maybe I should go?"

"No!" I say, so forcefully that he laughs. "No," I say again softer, this time moving two steps toward him and taking his right hand in mine. "Stay for a little while."

I'm embarrassed and excited at the same time, and there must have been a suggestive edge to my words, because now Luke blushes a little.

"Do you want to go upstairs?" he asks, squeezing my hand tighter.

"Yes, but..."

"But what?" he asks, bending a little to look curiously into my face.

At a loss for a gentler response, I just come out with it.

"But we're not doing..."

"Doing what? You mean *that*? Sex?"

He's still staring right at me as he says it, and now I'm the one turning red and feeling childish for even mentioning it.

"Yes, that's what I mean."

"I didn't think we were going to," he says, eyes holding steady. How is he so cool right now? Has he had this conversation a million times before? I'm about to respond when he interrupts me by adding, "At least not tonight."

My stomach flutters.

"Good, glad we're clear on that," I say, turning to head up to my room, still holding his hand.

Behind me, Luke says, "I did tell my parents that I'm spending the night at Adam's tonight."

Halfway up the stairs, I halt, and turn to face him.

"Are you serious?"

"Yes," he says, looking a little devious.

"Where are you planning to sleep?"

"In the van."

"Why?"

"Because I didn't know if you'd be out for the night. You and Jamie could have made up or something; you could have gone to her house. I thought I might need to stalk you a little harder," he says with a laugh.

A slow smile creeps across my face. The gesture is sweet: Luke risked getting in trouble with his parents and spending all night in his van just to try to win me back.

"Well, I'm sure my mom won't be home for a while. At least you can stay in the warm house until she comes back."

"Sounds good," Luke says as I turn and finish the climb, pulling my delinquent boyfriend behind me to the top of the stairs, down the hallway, and into my bedroom, and shutting the door behind us.

31

"Where did you park?" I whisper with a sudden sense of urgency as I listen to the garage door open and close downstairs.

"Down the street; I was stalking you, remember?"

"Get in the closet," I whisper back, making a snap decision that I hope I won't regret later.

"Are you serious? I can just go," he offers, but he's moving toward the closet as he speaks.

"No, I want you to stay. But hurry up; my mom will be upstairs in a minute," I say, simultaneously kicking a massive pile of notes under the bed and scanning the bedroom for any visible traces of boy.

I hear the sink running in the kitchen; she must be

getting a glass of water. Glancing at the clock, I wonder whether my mom will think it's weird if I'm asleep just after nine. Maybe. But I have no other way to get rid of her quickly, so I bolt across the room and throw myself under the covers. I try to breathe easier and look peaceful, even though my heart is racing.

Mom's footsteps are growing louder, and with only seconds left, I whisper a barely audible "shhh" to Luke.

I can't believe there's a boy in my closet right now! What am I thinking?

No time to ponder my stupidity. The door opens slowly and I freeze. I'm facing the wall, but I keep my eyes closed anyway, just in case she rushes over to check whether I'm faking.

Highly unlikely.

"Night, London, I love you." My mom's whispered words float through the night air so softly that they're barely there. Is this her nightly ritual? I can't help but feel a pang of guilt at the deceit that's happening under her nose.

Then again, she's been deceiving me for years.

After the door quietly taps the frame and I hear my mom slowly release the handle; after her footsteps disappear into her own room; after the water rushes to wash toothpaste and face soap down the drain; after the TV in her room sounds; after that, I wait five more excruciatingly long minutes.

And then I tiptoe to the closet.

"Hi," I whisper to Luke. It's pitch-black. I can't see anything.

From the back corner of the closet comes his smooth voice.

"Hi."

I hear him climb to his feet and watch his perfect self materialize from the darkness.

Instead of stopping, Luke walks until his warm body is pressing against mine in the closet doorway.

"Hi," he says again, even smoother this time, if that's possible, before planting a long and borderline inappropriate kiss on my lips.

Perhaps we're both charged by the exhilaration of being bad, or maybe it's the pitch-blackness that drives us, but soon enough we're on the floor of my walk-in and a few articles of clothing aren't exactly where they should be.

I stick to my earlier promise of not doing . . . that. But for at least an hour, maybe more, Luke makes it very, very difficult.

"I have to go to sleep," I say when my breathing has finally slowed to the point that I can speak. I'm lying on Luke's bare chest, which is strangely comfortable, considering it's hard as a rock.

"I know," he says softly, leaning down to kiss the top of my head before beginning to untangle his longer limbs from mine.

"Where's my shirt?" I ask, surprisingly at ease being literally and emotionally exposed to him.

"Here you go," he says, tossing it my way.

Once we're both dressed, Luke in what he wore this evening and me in pajamas, we walk toward my bed.

"Sleep here with me, okay?" I say.

"I think I'll take the floor in the closet," he says, adding, "just in case."

"No, she won't come in," I promise, without really knowing whether we'll be caught.

"How about this: I'll lie here until you fall asleep, then I'll go in the closet so she doesn't find me in the morning."

Too tired to argue, and anxious to be out before my memory resets at 4:33, I climb back in bed. This time, I scoot close to the wall and leave half the bed for Luke. He joins me under the covers and immediately we're snapped together like Legos.

"Crap," I mutter.

"What's wrong?"

"I need to write a note. I need to write this down or I'll forget."

"Yes, please do," Luke says. "I don't want you to freak out again and make me explain things to your mom."

"Very funny," I say, elbowing him. He laughs quietly and I do, too, remembering the note from the day after our first date. Luke read that note and many of the others earlier tonight.

"Hmm, just a sec," Luke says, reaching his outside arm toward the nightstand and retrieving my cell phone. He frees his other arm from under me, quickly types a message, and hits send. Immediately, my phone buzzes to alert me that I have a new text.

"What does it say?" I ask after Luke sets the phone back next to the bed.

"The boy in the closet is your boyfriend. He loves you and will tell you all about last night."

"Cute," I say, feeling my eyelids droop and sleep approach. "Don't forget to tell me about the last hour in the closet."

"I'll re-create it for you tomorrow," Luke says, pulling me closer and breathing in my hair. "I really do, you know."

"Do what?" I ask in a sleepy haze.

"I really do love you, London."

"I love you, too, Luke."

32

The text said there was a boy in my closet, but all I found is this note.

> Dear London,
>   You snore.
>   I heard your mom leave, so I escaped. I'll come back in a while with coffee and officially announce my presence. If she comes back, you might want to tell her I'm coming so she knows we're okay.
>   Read up...all of your notes are under your bed.
>   You were too tired to write a note last

night but here are the highlights (I'll fill in
the holes later):

   —I begged your forgiveness (you'll read
about why)
   —Thankfully, you forgave me
   —We spent hours reading your notes—
you said that was a great way for me to
get to know the real you
   —As previously mentioned, you snore...
and talk in your sleep
   —I promised to reenact certain...other
things

   Last night was amazing. I wish you could
remember it, but I'll do my best to remind
you. Oh, and PS—you are the best kisser
ever.

Love,
Luke

"Aren't we happy this morning?" my mom says when she
returns from the grocery store and sees my permagrin. I
stuff a bite of a bagel into my mouth, but it doesn't help,
so I just shrug in response.

"Dare I ask?" she says, which is really asking, isn't it?
Mom pours herself some coffee and leans against the
counter, gazing at me, mug in hand.

"Luke and I made up," I say matter-of-factly, once I've swallowed the biggest bite imaginable.

"Ahh, I see," she says with a knowing look.

"He's coming over this morning," I add, gesturing to my outfit as if it needed explanation. Every Saturday I can remember is spent in pajamas, until noon at least. "We're going to hang out today."

I think I see a touch of hurt flash across my mother's eyes, but in an instant, it's gone.

"That's great, London," she says, pushing off the countertop and topping off her cup. "Maybe I'll go into the office and catch up on some work, then."

"Sounds good," I say, thrilled that Luke and I might be alone in the house for a while. The notes I read painted a picture of a boy so appealing that I find myself wanting to be unsupervised. Except, of course, that he lied to me, but his note said we made up. I'll count on him to walk me through the evening minute by minute.

As if on cue, the doorbell rings, and I practically run to the entryway to answer it. Flinging it open, I nearly gasp at the boy standing there in the bright sun.

Sure, there were photos, but they didn't do him justice.

Luke is holding two to-go cups of coffee, but instead of coming in, he stands on the porch.

"Let's go," he says.

"Where?"

"You'll see."

Quickly, I run and tell Mom that we're going to the

mall—hey, it could be true—then grab my jacket, cell, and wallet. I return to find Luke gazing out toward the street. He hears my footsteps and turns to face me, eyes bright and beautiful.

"Ready?"

"Yep," I say, bounding out of the house and taking the coffee from his outstretched hand. He kisses me lightly on the cheek and whispers, "Did you get my note?"

"Yes," I say, and it comes out more intimate than I meant, but it feels just fine.

"Good," he says, in a way that makes me squirm. We walk to the van, buckle up, and pull out of the driveway, headed to who knows where.

And, honestly, I don't care.

Coffee in hand, highway before me, gorgeous boyfriend to my left, this day is bound to be good.

33

Eight hours later, under the setting sun, I'm standing at the cemetery entrance wondering how it came to this. The chill shooting down my spine makes me rethink my decision to head in alone. I gesture to Luke in the van, and he quickly kills the engine and appears at my side.

I grab his hand and it gives me the will to move.

The scene before me reminds me too much of the funeral in my notes and emblazoned in my brain, a vision now so confusing it hurts.

It was sweet of Luke to take me there, to Lingering Pines Retirement Community. He had read all about it last night and explained on the way that meeting my grandmother in person would be best. He had printed a map, and he bought travel snacks when he left my house. He'd also gone home to shower and change his clothes so that his parents wouldn't worry.

During the drive, Luke talked through every giggle-inducing, glow-generating, lust-inspiring detail of the night before. At times, I wanted to tell him to pull off the road so that I could jump across the center divider and have my way with him.

He told me about me: all the notes he'd read and thoughts he had about what my life must be like.

Luke talked about us meeting as kids, about being drawn to me from childhood. About the shoe game.

We chatted and sipped lattes and ate M&M's and peanut butter crackers, and I was calm and happy and loved.

But then we arrived.

What I saw of Lingering Pines was the reception desk, where a fat young nurse checked a computer and called her supervisor before pulling me aside to whisper in my face with onion breath that Jo Lane had in fact lived there for five years until she moved on.

"Where did she go?" I asked innocently, not getting it.

"I'm so sorry to be the one telling you this, but Jo passed last winter," the young nurse said. "She died," she added, probably because of my dazed look.

That's about the point when I felt myself being strapped onto a roller-coaster ride that I didn't stand in line for. After having the wherewithal to glean as much additional information as possible, Luke guided my stupefied self back to the van and drove me far away from Lingering Pines, never pressing too hard but letting me know he was there.

"I'm so sorry, London," he said.

"I didn't know her," I said back, my mind reeling. The miles flew by then. We were headed home, and I was not only empty-handed but downright mystified as well.

The questions in my mind were the same then and now.

How can she be dead? She's in my future. Am I wrong about the woman at the child's funeral? Is it someone who just looks like my grandma? I need to check that photo again. Maybe I should show it to my mom. Maybe my grandma has a sister. A twin sister.

Each thought stands in turn in front of my mind's eye for a mental audition, but no one gets the part. No thought is just right.

"Thanks for bringing me here," I say quietly, cutting through the silence as Luke and I move straight down the center aisle of the graveyard.

"No problem," Luke says softly. He keeps his eyes on the sea of stone going by. Our feet crunch on dirt and rocks as we walk, and I'm desperately trying to remain rational, to not picture zombies digging themselves up from underground or ghosts whispering in my ear.

Unsure of exactly what I'm looking for, my eyes instinctively seek the familiar: the groundskeeper's shack disguised as a mausoleum.

Tracking my gaze, Luke squeezes the hand he holds tight.

"That's where the smoking guy will be, right?" he asks. His simple question gives me a strange sense of calm. Belonging, even. From reading my life, Luke not only understands me, but he remembers, too. In a way, he has become the closest thing to a memory I might ever have.

"Yes," I say with a nod, keeping my eyes focused there.

I'm so absorbed that I see the movement from inside that anyone else might have missed in the dying light. "Let's go over," I say, pulling Luke off the main path and onto a smaller branch cutting through graves toward the shed. I lift my hand to knock, but the door opens before I get the chance.

"Good evening," says a cherub-faced man with a beard like Santa Claus's. "How can I help you kids?"

"Hi," I begin timidly, trying to find my words. "We're looking for a grave. My grandmother's grave, actually. I didn't know her, and we were wondering whether there's some sort of directory."

"A directory, huh? The only directory you'll find here is locked in my noggin," the man says with a kind smile and a tap, forefinger to temple. "My mind is like a steel trap: it never lets anything out. What was your grandmother's name?"

I glance at Luke before turning back to Santa.

"Jo Lane," I say.

"She died last winter," Luke offers.

Santa scratches his head, muttering, "Lane...Lane, hmm..." I watch; the caretaker seems familiar to me. Maybe it's just that he looks like Santa Claus.

Luke and I catch gazes again, and just as I'm wondering whether Santa's brain isn't as advertised, his weathered face brightens.

"I've got it. Aisle thirteen, plot two hundred forty-seven. Or is it two hundred forty-eight? Follow me, please." He steps onto the path and leads us in the opposite direction from which we came. We follow, farther away from the safety of the main walkway, right into the thick of death.

As Luke and I gingerly step behind the crunch, crunch, crunch of Santa's work boots, at least one of us wonders about the sanity of someone who chooses to work at a cemetery. As he moves, Santa mutters under his breath about Jo Lane's funeral.

"Sad turnout, that one. Only just the man and the priest. Poor woman."

Blameless, I'm guilty just the same.

I'm preoccupied by the eeriness of the passing graves, now that it's officially dark outside. Low-hanging trees make it even darker. It feels like the dead of night, even though it's barely six thirty.

Abruptly, the caretaker stops moving, and Luke grabs my waist to keep me from running into the old man.

"Here she is, two hundred thirty-seven," Santa says, gesturing to the simple rectangular granite grave marker at his feet. I can't help but think that he's standing on my grandmother.

"Thank you," I whisper, edging closer to the stone.

"No trouble," Santa says, turning back toward the shed. "Take your time; I'll close up when you leave."

I hear his boots crunch away as my eyes lock on the piece of stone like it's going to grow a mouth and tell me all the answers.

WIFE, MOTHER, GRANDMOTHER, FRIEND
JOSEPHINE LONDON LANE
JULY 10, 1936—DECEMBER 10, 2009

Tears sting my eyes for a woman I never knew. My namesake, apparently. Luke wraps his arm around my shoulders and pulls me close to his chest.

"You okay?" he asks.

"I don't know," I answer truthfully. I feel like I'm outside the scene, watching it unfold instead of living it.

We stand there a short while, and when it feels right, I take a step back.

"Let's go," I say to Luke.

He quietly leads me back the way we came, through

the graves and toward the caretaker's shed. It's impossible for me not to picture the darkness: I can see the younger, handsome, and seemingly out of place groundskeeper smoking now, consoling me from afar. In my memory, I'm looking at him from the direction we're now facing. In my memory, I am standing way over . . .

My heart leaps and my feet stop as I see it: the green stone angel who cries that day in the future.

Luke turns to face me and asks what's wrong. Instead of answering, I take off running.

"London?" Luke calls after me.

I hear him running, too; I'm reassured by the heavy thud of his steps in my wake. At least if I hit a tree or encounter a ghost, he'll find me quickly.

My North Star in the expanse of graves, the crying angel stands tall above her silent neighbors, keeping watch in the night.

As I approach, the butterflies in my stomach breed and multiply in fast-forward. My side aches from sprinting, and vomit threatens to rise in my throat. I don't know if it's the exertion or the anticipation that's making me feel sick, but I swallow hard to keep it at bay.

Soon enough, I am at the angel's base. Instead of lingering, I turn in the direction I remember, facing the location of the funeral in my mind.

Instead of the nothing I expect — the vacant plot waiting for the helpless being, the child — there is something.

Slowly, trying to catch my breath, I creep toward it,

my mind clicking and spinning and working on the problem it can't seem to sort out. Until there it is.

The answer.

I find myself standing in the exact spot as in my dark memory, facing not a freshly dug hole but a tasteful, polished headstone surrounded by mature plantings. Light from the street lamp outside the iron fence bounces just right; I can read the ornate lettering plain as day.

I swallow back bile as Luke stomps up next to me. At least I think it's Luke. I don't turn to check.

"I lost you back there for a second," his familiar voice pants as he catches his breath.

Staring, I'm not sure whether I'm still breathing at all.

I stand motionless, eyes locked on the letters. Out of my peripheral vision, I see Luke read them, too, then glance up toward the groundskeeper's shack in the distance and to the green angel to the left.

"Wait, is this..." His voice trails off midquestion, and, finally, he joins me in the realization. "Whoa," is all my boyfriend says, before taking my hand and staring right along with me.

When the groundskeeper approaches and scolds us for running through the cemetery and disturbing the peace, I turn to realize that it is him.

He's older now, fatter and bearded, but were he smiling in sympathy instead of scowling and annoyed, he would look the same. I can see now what I couldn't see before: I can see him beneath the years.

Luke and I grudgingly agree to leave, but not before I take one last long, hard look at the engraving that will derail my life forever.

SWEET BABY BOY
JONAS DYLAN LANE
NOVEMBER 7, 1998—MAY 8, 2001

34

It punches me in the gut once more, just like the first time I read it and the time after that.

The funeral was in the past.

The past.

And I remember it.

I was so focused on the who that I completely missed the when.

Walking toward the cemetery gates, my head spins so much it aches. Inside the van, Luke cranks the heat and we begin to defrost as we drive in silence toward my house. I am paralyzed by emotion. Not until we exit the freeway and turn left into my development does Luke speak.

"You have to talk to your mom," he says.

I watch the houses that I remember from tomorrow go by and wonder whether a part of me remembers them from yesterday, too. All the rules to my world are being challenged with this one discovery. The simplicity of knowing what's coming isn't so simple after all.

I find myself wanting to call Jamie. Wishing I could. I shake off the thought and watch the houses some more.

As Luke pulls into my driveway, the porch light blinks on. I glance at the dashboard clock and realize that it's nearly eight o'clock, which is not so strange, except that I left before eleven this morning and haven't called since.

"She must be worried." Luke says what I'm thinking.

"She should be," I say.

"Go easy on her."

"I'll try," I reply weakly before I slide out of the van and head inside to confront my mother and discover the truth about my missing memories.

35

"Who was Jonas?" I ask again, somehow guessing the answer but needing confirmation.

My mother's eyes share a mixture of shock and sorrow that makes me want to look away.

But I don't.

"Who was he, Mom?" I ask a third time, softer now.

"How do you know..." She looks down at her hands. I stay still, watching her realize that how doesn't matter.

Mom lifts her gaze once more, but though her head is high now, her posture has cracked.

"Jonas was your brother," she says in a near whisper.

I am silent, unable to ask her to go on, but she does anyway.

"He died."

"I know. I was at the cemetery. I saw his tombstone."

"Why..." She stops herself. "Well, that part doesn't matter."

"I'll tell you how I ended up there after you tell me what happened to my brother," I say, a tear racing down my cheek, "and why you lied about him. Lied about me."

"Oh, London, I didn't lie. I kept a very sad truth from you. I thought..."

"What, that I should be blissfully stupid my whole life?"

"That I could save you the pain," Mom says, touching her hand to her cheek in anticipation of tears to come. I can see that I've exposed an old wound. A very deep, painful one.

"Something terrible happened to him a long time ago," Mom begins, glancing at me every so often but mostly watching the patterns in the carpet, as if they're feeding her lines. "Your brother was taken. And killed."

I inhale sharply. "Who did it?"

"We never knew."

My mother's shoulders are heaving now, and I'm the parent for a moment as I walk over to the couch and hold her in my arms. She cries on my shoulder for a brother I can't remember.

I want to know more, but I can see that talking about it is devastating to her.

When she composes herself, she pulls back, hands on my shoulders.

"I wasn't trying to deceive you, London, you have to know that," she says, looking right into me. "You lost your memory of the past, and I saw that as the one bright spot in all the darkness. You wouldn't have to know the pain of loss. I could protect you from it. That's what I've tried to do all these years."

When she says it like that, though I may not agree, I can understand. A little.

I break free from my mother's grasp and move to one of the cushiony chairs opposite the TV. I fold my legs up under me, even though I'm still wearing the shoes that carried me through the cemetery.

The notes told me that my mom has been keeping secrets, but I've been keeping them, too. It's time to come clean.

To ask for help.

"Mom?"

"Yes, sweetie?"

"I want to know all about Jonas. I know it's hard for you, but I want you to tell me everything. It's important."

I grab the tops of my shoes and pull my feet closer to my body.

"I know it is, London. I know you want to understand your life."

Taking a deep breath, I look into my mom's dark eyes.

For the first time, I understand the tinge of anguish that will always be there, even during happy occasions.

I don't remember him. I don't remember anything. But she remembers all of it.

"Mom, it's more than wanting to understand. I think I need to hear about him. I think it might help me."

"What do you mean?" she asks, confused.

Finally, I share with my mom what's been building, what I know from notes that I've kept from the one person I should have opened up to long ago.

"I want you to tell me everything, because I think it might help me remember my past," I say.

My mother sighs and rubs her eyes.

"London, you've been to doctors who have tried to jog your memory. I even took you to a hypnotist once. Why do you think that my telling you the story of your brother's death will change things now?"

And here it is: the moment of truth. I check the clock on the wall for no particular reason. Then I shift in my seat, and pull myself tighter into a knot. I take a deep breath, and, finally, I tell my mother what she needs to hear.

"Mom, I remember Jonas's funeral."

Written 2/19; include in notes every night.

This morning I woke up remembering a memory I'm sure will stay with me forever. It's a funeral...it was my brother Jonas's. It's the one past memory I have.

Mom kept it from me for years. She wanted to protect me. It's hard not to be mad at her, but I try not to be. She didn't think I needed the pain on top of the stress of the memory thing. She has to live with it every day and didn't want me to have to, too.

Mom wasn't there when it happened but told me the story. Jonas and I were with Dad. I was six and Jonas was two. We were at the grocery store and Dad went over to get a cart. He left us in the car alone for two minutes. He just walked across the parking lot, and when he came back, Jonas was gone.

I guess Dad told Mom I was screaming about a van and pointing at one leaving the parking lot, so Dad jumped in the car and chased it. She said it's all he could do. But after a couple of blocks, the van made a light that turned red as Dad and I approached. He tried to floor it. There was an accident. Mom says our car was demolished; I was hurt pretty badly. I was in a coma, and early one morning, at 4:33 a.m., I died. Obviously, they brought me back, but Mom thinks that's why my brain resets then.

After that, apparently my normal memory was gone. I didn't remember the accident. I didn't remember Jonas.

Mom kicked Dad out. She blamed him for losing Jonas and seriously hurting me. He probably blamed himself, too.

I asked Mom about the birthday cards from Dad in the manila folder in the desk drawer. I found them in her closet last fall. She was a little mad about the snooping, but she said that Dad tried to get in touch three times, but each time she told him to leave us alone. She explained that she was very bitter then. She just seems sad now. Maybe Mom and Dad should talk. I might need to talk to Dad, too.

Two years after he was kidnapped, police found a few of Jonas's bones and his clothes in the mountains west of town. We buried him then. That's the funeral I remember.

I'm writing this down so I can leave it for myself every night. I know it will be hard to read each morning, but it's important. I owe it to Jonas.

I owe it to my brother to remember him.

36

By all accounts, it's a beautiful April morning.

Tomorrow is Monday, so today is the weekend.

I sit on a swivel chair at the glass-top table on the patio, drinking a latte that my mom made unprompted. The sun is up on the other side of the house, so I sit in the shade with a light breeze rustling my unkempt hair.

I'm still wearing pajamas—a supersoft T-shirt and lightweight drawstring shorts—with fuzzy fleece slippers that I don't remember breaking in on my feet.

I've just finished a delicious toasted bagel with cream cheese, and I've just read through a pile of notes about a megawonderful boy named Luke. Apparently I've been dating him for almost six months. It's too nice a day to dwell on the fact that I don't seem to remember him, backward or forward.

I sigh, in the manner of Snow White before the whole apple thing, and pick up the other letter that was left on the nightstand this morning. It is weathered and smudged, and I can't help but wonder how many mornings I've read the words before me now.

Sighing again, I shake my hair out of my face, take a slow sip of latte, and smooth the page. The words hit me like a sledgehammer.

Tears upon tears splat onto the lined pages in my hands as I discover a nightmare come true. Quickly, I wipe away the salt water so it won't fade the ink. Because even as my chest caves in and makes me hate the chipper birds and everything else, I know that I needed to read this today, and I need to read it again tomorrow.

For me, reading is remembering.

37

"Does it ever get easier?" I ask my mom before I open the door to the Prius. We are sitting in the drop-off area at school. My eyes are red and puffy.

"I don't know, London," my mom says softly, placing a hand on mine. "For me, time lessens the pain. I don't know how it will be for you. It's new to you every day."

My mother looks tormented as she says this. I don't answer. She hesitates like she wants to say something, like she's debating with herself. The side that wants to speak wins.

"Sweetie, I think you should consider getting rid of that letter," she says carefully.

"No."

"London, think about it. Jonas wouldn't want you to be so hurt on his behalf every morning. He wouldn't want you to grieve for him anew each day."

"How do you know? He was a baby."

"A happy baby! A baby who giggled constantly and made you laugh and was your biggest fan. I'll show you the videos again, if you'd like."

"There are videos?"

"Of course, London," Mom says quietly. "Anyway, the point is that I know his little soul wouldn't want his big sister to be so miserable."

I unbuckle my seat belt and open the door, ready to go inside.

"I feel like I owe it to him," I say quietly. "To remember him today and every other day." I'm quoting myself from the note I read this morning, but it's how I feel.

My mother sighs deeply. A car beeps behind us and I know I need to get out. I know I need to go have my normal day at school.

My mom glares at the impatient parent in the car behind us, then looks back at me. Her hand is still on mine.

"Why, London?" she asks. "Why do you owe it to him?"

I pull back my hand and open the car door. With one foot out on the pavement, school bag in hand, I say to my mother, "Because I'm alive and he's not."

*   *   *

"Ms. Lane? Uh, Ms. Lane? Excuse me? London Lane, are you in there?"

I look up to find two rows of gawking students and a slightly agitated Mr. Hoffman staring at me expectantly.

I completely missed the question, but after a quick glance at the board, I know what he asked.

"F prime," I mutter, thankful that I managed to remember the benign parts of this morning's briefing in addition to those very, very cancerous ones that were distracting me in the first place.

"Very good, Ms. Lane. Feel free to zone out again," Mr. Hoffman says, with a wink that tries too hard to be cool.

Poor Mr. Hoffman. He will never succeed.

A girl with poodle hair in front of me leans back so far in her creaky, overused chair that her locks rest on the pages of my open notebook. The tangled tresses obscure nothing, since I've taken no notes. My blank notepad and mechanical pencil are props, like the backpack in the basket below my seat and, quite frankly, the schoolbooks inside of it.

I brush her hair off my paper anyway, and she twists around with a stern look on her face. She combs her fingers through her hair as the bell rings.

I gather my things and head toward the door of the classroom, then merge into the swarm of students buzzing from this class to that one.

When I make it to my locker, I see Jamie across the hallway, standing on her own. I adjust the metal door so I can see her reflection in the mirror.

Jamie shuffles a few books around, then sets her bag on the floor and grabs a lip gloss off the top shelf. After carefully applying it, she hoists her bag on her shoulder and slams her locker shut.

She turns in my direction and hesitates. Just as I think she's going to come talk to me, she turns on her heels and walks off down the hall. When she's gone, I slam my own locker shut and follow her, twenty paces behind, wishing all the way we were arm in arm.

Jamie is eyeing me suspiciously across our desk island. We're supposed to be working together to create a ficti-tious travel itinerary for a two-week vacation in Mexico. It's busywork, and normally I'd be all for it.

Later in life, I'll do a lot of traveling. But today, I'm not interested.

"What?" I hiss at her. I'm not in the mood.

"Nothing," she says, taken aback by my atypically harsh response.

I pull the Mexico travel guide toward me and ran-domly open it to the section on Isla de Mujeres. I can't help but laugh. I remember being there. With Jamie. A slightly more weathered but still gorgeous Jamie.

Flipping through the hotels section, I come across photos that give me the sense of déjà vu. A hotel on a private island, surrounded by the clearest, bluest ocean imaginable.

It reminds me of Luke's eyes, staring into me this morning in study hall.

I can't help but smile more broadly.

"What's so funny?" Jamie asks bitingly.

"Nothing, this hotel just looks nice," I say, turning the book to show her.

I wonder whether right now I'm planting our getaway idea deep in my subconscious. I wonder whether somehow a little piece of me will remember today when Jamie and I finally do plan the trip.

"I guess." Jamie is shrugging, looking at the glorious hotel. "I've seen better."

I take back the book and start working on our assignment. Jamie sits quietly for a few seconds, then surprises me with a question.

"Are you okay?" she asks.

I look up at her.

"I'm fine, why?"

"You look like you've been crying," she practically whispers, checking to make sure no one else is eavesdropping. I like that she's concerned about embarrassing me.

"Yeah," I say, shrugging myself this time. "I've had some stuff going on."

"Oh," Jamie says, looking down at her lap. For a moment, I think my memory is wrong, that it won't take another few weeks for us to make up. But then, as quick as it was there, Jamie's compassion is gone.

"The period is halfway over. Give me that. I'll do it," she says, grabbing the book from me. Immediately, she goes to work on a faux itinerary for a trip that she doesn't know she'll eventually take . . . with me.

As I watch my best friend work on our joint assignment alone, I feel strangely invigorated. I know she wants to ask me what's wrong. I know she cares that I'm upset. I know she misses me.

And knowing all that motivates me.

I'll get my best friend back.

But first, I'll break up the relationship that will do nothing but cause her heartache.

38

"Where are we going?" Luke asks.

"Just drive," I say. "Turn left at the light."

Luke does as I instruct, and then protests. "I thought you wanted to hang out after school. Not go on a stakeout."

"Funny," I say. I point as I command, "Turn right and then slow down. I need to look for the house number."

Written on a scrap of paper is 1553 Mountain Street. It's amazing what you can find in the phone book.

"There it is," I say, reflexively ducking down in my seat. "The white one on the right. The one with the black shutters. Pass it and park down the street."

Luke shakes his head but does as I ask. He pulls the van into a spot and puts it in park. I reach over and turn down the radio, even though it's already low. Then I turn it off.

"They'd have to have bionic ears to have heard that, you know," Luke laughs.

"Shhh," I say to him, craning my neck to see the house behind us.

"Here, try this," Luke says, flipping down the passenger-side visor and revealing a mirror. I adjust it and see the house without turning my head.

"Thanks," I say quietly.

"Sure," he says, looking at me curiously. "So, what now? What are we doing?"

"Watching the house," I say.

"For what?" Luke asks.

"The Messenger," I reply.

"The Messenger," he repeats flatly, leaning back in his seat and staring out the window at nothing.

A car pulls into a driveway a few houses in front of us, and a woman struggles to carry two armfuls of bags inside. The wind doesn't want her to make it. It blinds her with her own hair and presses against her shoulders.

I try to explain the situation to Luke.

"I need to figure out who Mr. Rice's wife tutors," I say.

"How do you know she's a tutor?" Luke asks.

I roll my eyes at him and reply, "Because I do. Jesse Henson will tell me next year that Mrs. Rice is a better math tutor than Ms. Hanover is a teacher."

"Who is Jesse Henson?" Luke asks, totally missing the point.

"Just a girl in my math class next year," I say, annoyed. "She'll sit next to me. She's chatty."

"So, what, you want to find out who Mrs. Rice tutors now so you can tell that kid about her husband?" Luke asks, finally seeing the light.

I nod once.

"But won't the person just tell Mrs. Rice it was you who told?" Luke asks, confused.

"Not if I'm smart," I say.

"I see," he says, and I wonder whether he means it. Luke strums his hands on the steering wheel like he's bored.

Nothing is happening at the Rice house, and I'm growing less and less excited about my mission by the second.

Sighing, I change the subject.

"What do you think of hypnotism?" I ask.

"Honestly, I don't think about it," Luke says, looking at me now with his soft blue eyes.

"Well, do for a minute. Do you think that I could be hypnotized to remember more?"

"More what? Past or future?"

"Either one," I say, but I don't really mean it. Remembering the future feels normal to me. The one past memory in my brain is like a splinter. It doesn't belong.

"Maybe a hypnotist could jog your memory about me," Luke mutters, looking back to the street.

"Maybe," I say, focusing again on the house behind

me. "Wouldn't it be nice to date someone who remembers you every morning?"

"Sure," Luke says. "Then again, maybe you'd get bored with me."

"No way," I reply. "So, what do you think?"

"I think it's up to you," Luke answers. His noncommittal comment bugs me. I glance his way to roll my eyes at him, and then I look back at the house.

Still nothing.

"I want whatever you want, as far as your brain is concerned. I love you no matter what," Luke says, and when I turn to face him, our eyes lock.

I wonder whether my heart keeps time even when my head doesn't. Maybe that's why I feel so much for Luke right now, even though I technically just met him this morning in study hall.

Something catches my eye and ruins the moment. A white car zips past us, and I can only assume that it's being driven by someone who can't see the future dangers of reckless driving.

It turns without slowing into the driveway in front of the white house with the black shutters: 1553 Mountain Street.

The Messenger has arrived.

I wait excitedly as the person turns off the car, gets organized, and opens the door. Forgoing the mirror, I turn in my seat to get a better look just as long blonde hair appears from the car.

I focus and then groan.

The Messenger is Carley Lynch, making things a touch more complicated. Originally, I was just going to "encourage" the Messenger to stumble upon Jamie and Mr. Rice. Now, with Carley involved, I need to modify the plan.

Carley Lynch would never take a suggestion from me.

"What are you going to do?" Luke asks an hour later, tossing a small decorative pillow up in the air and catching it over and over again. I want to grab the pillow and throw it out the window.

"I don't know," I say, remembering plenty of instances when Carley will make her feelings known, ranging from times she'll merely scowl at me to those special occasions when she'll bitingly comment on my clothes, walk, or general existence.

"Can't you just remember what you'll do and do that?" Luke presses, still tossing the stupid pillow.

"Luke!" I shout at him. "Do you think I'd be worrying about this if I remembered how to solve it? My memories of Jamie and Mr. Rice end much later, and very badly. What I'm trying to do now is change all that. I'm flying blind here, buddy. Perhaps you could help me out a little instead of playing catch with that stupid pillow."

Just then, Luke's most recent toss lands in his hands, and instead of releasing it again, he sets the pillow aside.

"Sorry," he says, sitting up and looking right at me. "Come sit down."

"I don't want to," I say, like a mad little girl. But somehow, Luke's sweet eyes and gentle smile sand off my rough edges. Soon enough, I'm lounging with him on my bed, brainstorming the path that will lead to the premature demise of Jamie's affair.

We're still on my bed when my mom knocks once and comes into my room at 9:45. She's home late, and, frankly, I'd forgotten about her. I'd forgotten about dinner and time and everything else.

"Oh, Luke!" Mom says. She looks at him splayed out on top of the covers.

"We're hatching a plan," I explain when she shoots a warning glance my way. It's not much of an explanation, but it's all I've got.

"That's nice, but why don't you continue this tomorrow? It's getting late," she says.

"What time is it?" Luke asks, leaning over so that he can see the clock on the nightstand.

"Almost ten," Mom answers.

Quickly, Luke scoots to the edge of the bed and throws on his shoes.

"I gotta go," he says. "My mom's going to freak."

Luke stands and then squats down in front of me and kisses me on the lips right in front of my mom.

Gutsy. I like it.

Then he throws on his jacket, waves good-bye to both of us, and hurries out of the room. I hear him bound down the stairs and out the door, closing it with a slam behind him.

"Sorry," I say to my mom when we're alone. "I didn't realize how late it got."

"It's okay, sweetie," she says, smoothing my hair. "Luke is a good guy."

"Yeah, I really like him," I say. "I think I love him."

I wonder whether my mom is going to give me a lecture on young love and chastity and all that humiliating stuff, but she doesn't. Instead, she surprises me by saying simply, "I know you do."

After a hug, she leaves me alone in my room feeling happy about the day and wishing that I could hold on to it forever.

Instead, I get to work. Without Luke's hotness to distract me, and with the help of my notes, I brainstorm. In the end, it's crystal clear: I'll make the gossip superhighway work for me.

With the unwitting assistance of Gabby Stein, future valedictorian Christopher Osborne, Alex Morgan, and, ultimately, Carley Lynch, I'll save Jamie.

That is, if all the dominoes fall as they should.

39

Following detailed instructions from this morning's note, I shove the folded paper into Gabby Stein's locker seconds before students start arriving to dress down for gym. Without being too obvious about it, I watch Gabby find the note, read it, and blush.

In that moment, I know that domino number one will fall: Gabby will go to the Driver's Ed. room at lunch looking for Christopher. Unless there is some uncontrollable coincidence, he obviously won't be there. But I know from notes that Jamie and Mr. Rice will be.

That's gossip too rich for Gabby to keep to herself.

Five periods later, I arrive early to Brit. Lit., anxiously

awaiting the arrival of Gabby and my next domino, the evil Alex Morgan.

Gabby shows first, and I know by looking at her that she saw them. She's practically bursting with her new-found secret. I try to hide my excitement as Gabby furiously whispers to Alex the second she arrives. Then, before the bell—before Ms. Jenkins can remind her about the "no texting in class" rule—Alex types and sends a message on her cell phone that I can only hope is meant for Carley.

After school, I ask Luke to drive me to an address from this morning's note.

"Again?" he asks.

"Guess so." I shrug.

Luke drives but doesn't seem happy about it. When we arrive, he pulls into a space down the block and points to the house in question. In minutes, a white car zips into the driveway. Carley Lynch gets out.

"What are you looking for this time?" Luke asks.

I squint to be sure, and then I answer.

"That," I say, pointing.

"What? Carley?"

"Not Carley. Her *expression*. Her posture. She looks worried."

"So?" Luke asks. "You think that means she knows?"

I take a deep breath and let it out, relieved. It's a small victory.

"Yes," I tell my boyfriend. "She knows."

"Now what?" he asks.

I look him in the eyes, so glad to have him in my life.

"Let's go," I say.

"That's it? That's all we came for? To see Carley's expression?"

"Yep," I say.

"You aren't going to do anything else?"

"Nope. Don't have to."

Luke shakes his head at me as he starts the ignition and pulls out of the parking space.

"Seems like a waste of time," he mutters.

"I hope it wasn't," I say quietly.

"For Jamie's sake, me, too," Luke replies. "I just can't believe that's all you're going to do."

"Well, there is one other thing," I say.

"What's that?" Luke asks.

"I'm going to forget this ever happened."

40

There is a cop car in the Meridan High School roundabout this morning. It's not something you see every day. Students are whispering; Carley Lynch's friends are consoling her at the top of the main hall.

It's all a bit unnerving.

When I arrive at Spanish, I find that Jamie is already there, leaning on top of her desk with her chin on her arms. She looks like she's been crying.

"What's the matter, J?" I ask softly as I sit down next to her.

"What do you think?" she asks, without looking at me.

I think forward to whispers about Jamie in the hallway. To a hostile courtroom. A testimony. A conviction.

I lie.

"I don't know, Jamie, but seriously, fight or not, you can talk to me. I'm always here for you."

Jamie looks at me with red eyes and a puffy face. The bell rings, and Ms. Garcia starts a Spanish-language movie. A few minutes in, Jamie turns to face me again.

"We got caught," she whispers. Fresh tears well up in her eyes. "The police took him away this morning. That bitch Carley Lynch told the principal. I'm sure it's the best news you've heard all day."

I hold her gaze for a while and then whisper back.

"It's not," I say honestly. "I'm so sorry, Jamie."

She looks away and doesn't speak for a moment. Then, finally, she does.

"I don't believe you," Jamie whispers, so softly I barely hear. Her chin sinks back to her arms.

I remember notes telling me Jamie's rule about sharing her future. If there will ever be a time to break the rules, it's now.

"Jamie," I whisper, "it's all going to work out okay. I promise."

Luke and I hold hands as we cut across the parking lot at lunch. There's a strange absence of wind, and it makes me feel even more unsettled than I already do. It's too calm for the turbulent day.

"I can't believe they got caught," I say to Luke as we climb into his van.

"Uh-huh," he says with a funny look on his face.

"What?" I ask.

"Nothing," he says.

"I feel really bad for her. I mean, I read my notes; I was pretty upset about their thing. But I can't believe he's going to jail. And poor Jamie. She has to go to court. And everyone is going to make fun of her. I remember it."

"There are worse things you could remember," Luke says.

"There are worse things I *do* remember," I say back, recalling the note about my brother this morning. Right now Jamie's mistake doesn't seem so big.

"Good thing it's the end of the year," I say.

"Why?" Luke asks as we pull out of the lot.

"It'll die down by next year," I report. "Jamie's going to be back to normal by then. Mostly."

I sigh the heavy sigh of knowing what's to come.

"It's nice out," Luke says, changing the subject. "Would a picnic make you feel better?"

"Yes," I say, imagining lying in the grass, staring at him all lunch period. "Yes, I think it would."

"Want to ask Jamie to come with us?" Luke offers.

"You're so sweet," I say. "That's a great idea." I pull out my phone and text the invitation; Jamie immediately writes back. Progress.

Home for lunch; forgot a book. Thanks though. Really. It means a lot.

I smile and text back. *Anytime, J.*

"Is she coming?" Luke asks.

"Nope, it's just us."

Ten minutes later, I'm waiting for Luke in his minivan in the grocery store parking lot while he buys food.

I wish he'd hurry up.

The springtime sun beats down on me through the windshield, and the heat and the stillness slow my breathing, relax my muscles, and muddy my focus. I'm in a daze as I watch a young mother carry her baby inside the store and come out a few minutes later with a box of diapers. A tall man and a short woman rush through the automatic doors, the man checking his watch as he walks. Two children, seemingly without supervision, run through the parking lot and into the store. I wonder where their mother is as I roll my heavy head to the left.

A face in the van window yanks me back to reality.

In a minute, I will realize that the woman is probably the mother of the two rambunctious boys I've just seen. In a minute, I'll note that her van in the next space over nearly matches Luke's, and that she was "just checking out the newer model," as she'll shout to me as a means of explanation. In a minute, my pulse will edge back down to resting.

But right now, I am rigid. I am terrified of the woman's big face, flanked by hands cupped so she can see inside the tinted windows. Right now, I am irrationally locking the doors and scooting my body away so that the stranger won't get me.

Stranger?

Get me?

Even as I think it, I know it's crazy.

But then something falls into place.

I see myself as a little girl. My dad is across the lot, pulling a cart from the return. I'm in the backseat. A toddler is strapped in across from me. It's my brother, Jonas. I'm playing peekaboo with him. He's giggling.

A woman knocks on the window on my side. She seems friendly. She has a nice smile. "I'm a friend of your mommy's," I hear her say through the glass. "Open the door so I can say hi," she says sweetly. "You can see my puppy," she says, holding open a big bag with a tiny dog inside.

I love dogs, especially tiny ones.

I unbuckle my belt. As I climb over the seat to the front, I see my dad over there with the carts. It's fine. He's nearby. He'll be happy to see my mommy's friend, too.

Like I do when I pretend to drive in the garage, I hit the locks. They all click.

Before I see the man, I hear Jonas scream. He doesn't like strangers. I turn around to see the man taking him out of his car seat. Jonas doesn't like it; he's crying and kicking.

Then his cries are getting quieter because he's going away.

"Daddy!" I scream as I watch my mommy's friend and the man put Jonas in a van. I'm never supposed to get out in a parking lot but I do anyway. "Daddy!" I scream and scream until he hears me and runs.

Daddy listens to what happened and drives fast and chases the van, but we hit a car and that's all I remember.

Tears are running down my cheeks when Luke rejoins me in the car.

"Take me home," I say quietly, and he does.

41

"Are you all right?" Mom says as she rushes toward me. When she reaches the chair where I'm curled in a ball, wrapped in a woven blanket and otherwise attempting to shield myself from the world, the back of her hand instinctively flits to my forehead.

"I don't have a fever," I say, shaking her off. "I'm fine, I just need your help."

She takes a step back in her business suit and heels and looks at me warily.

"Okay . . ." she says.

"We have to go to the police," I say matter-of-factly, my voice slightly muffled since the blanket has crept up toward my mouth. I push it away and sit up.

"Why on earth would we—"

"I know who did it. I know who took Jonas. I remember them."

I'm not surprised by the look of shock on my mother's face.

"Them?"

"Yes, them. A man and a woman. I can see them. I can help the police find them."

"Slow down, sweetie," my mom says, sitting on the couch to my right. "Tell me what happened."

I do, and the tears are unleashed again. It's all my fault.

"Honey, it's okay," my mom whispers, reaching over and stroking my hair. "You didn't do anything wrong."

"Yes, I did!" I wail. "I unlocked the doors! It's my fault he's gone. It's my fault he's dead!"

I pull the blanket back to my face and cry until there's nothing left.

"Shhh," my mom says, over and over, and I feel like shaking off her kindness. I don't deserve it. How can she still love me, knowing I'm the reason Jonas is dead?

Will she still love me when she hears the rest of the story?

"Mom, that's not all," I say through my tears. As terrible as the past memory is, it's done. What I haven't shared is the part in the future that hasn't happened yet. It weighs on me so heavily that I sink lower into the chair.

"What is it, London?" Mom says in a hushed tone,

brushing back my hair and wiping away my tears as they're replaced by new ones. "You can tell me anything."

Desperate to tell someone, I open my mouth and creak out the words.

"Luke is going to die, too."

In a voice so low that my mom has to crouch to hear me, I tell her the future memory that seeing the criminals' faces has triggered.

I tell her that it must be in five or six years, judging by my reflection in the storefront window on a city street I don't recognize. Luke is there.

I'm clutching a torn piece of paper with an address scrawled on it. We're watching, until someone emerges. We're curious. We plan to tell the police.

A man leaves the brownstone; he's wearing knockoff dress shoes and a blazer so that he doesn't look like a kidnapper and a killer, but then and now, I know the truth.

The man veers off the cobblestones to a side street, then again into an alley. We follow without meaning to, and, with just a couple of wrong turns, the bustling city that felt safe doesn't seem that way anymore. Luke and I turn back, but it's too late.

The man knows we're there.

"What gives?" he shouts at us. He seems drunk or high. He's definitely unstable.

We say nothing for a moment. Then, like that idiot in a horror movie, words that I want to vacuum back in fly out of my mouth.

"You took my brother," I blurt with false conviction.

"London," Luke whispers harshly, squeezing the hand he's holding. Luke is sensible.

"That's what you think, huh?" the man says, edging closer to us.

I know with every fiber of my being that we're in the worst kind of danger. This was the wrong move.

The man is chewing a toothpick, tossing it side to side in his mouth like he doesn't have a care in the world.

Instinctively, Luke takes a step forward as if to shield me. The man is no more than ten feet from us.

"Let's get out of here," I say quietly to Luke. I'm terrified. I step back and tug on his hand.

Without warning, the man reaches around his back, up and under his jacket, his right hand emerging heavy.

He has a gun.

I shiver as I describe this part to my mom, and she moves to the very edge of the couch so that she can touch my knee for support.

My cell phone buzzes as a text comes through, and I know without looking that it's Luke. I ignore it.

"Go on, it's okay," she encourages me.

I tell her that the man points the gun at us and holds it steady. Of course the murderer has a gun. How could we be so stupid?

"I can't let you leave now, can I?" the man asks, eyes narrow and dark.

He takes another step, gun still pointed, and Luke must

know what's coming, because at that moment, he does something heroic. Or stupid.

Luke drops my hand, shoves me away toward the mouth of the alley, and shouts, "London, run!" at the top of his lungs.

And I try.

But the bullets stop me.

My mom's hands are covering her mouth now as I tell her the rest: the world going silent after the shots stop; the rhythmic footfalls of the man fleeing the scene; the minutes when I believe I'm dying, lying faceup staring at a starless city sky. The guttural groans that pull me from my trance and drag me toward my dying boyfriend.

I pause to take a few deep breaths and then tell my mom about Luke's final moments. No last words. No sentiments. Just Luke, gasping for air, raw terror in his eyes.

42

I blubber my way through the end of the story, nose running, eyes overflowing, shoulders heaving. It's contagious, and my mom and I cry together for the past and the future.

When there are no more tears, my mom startles me by standing and slapping her thighs as she rises.

"Get up," she commands me. I am now so buried in the cushions someone might mistake me for furniture.

"Get up, London," she says again.

"I can't," I whisper.

"Yes, you can," she says, leaning over to help me. When she finds one of my hands, she grabs tight and tugs. I can't help but stand.

"You were right, we need to go to the police," she

says, drying my cheeks with her hands. "You were right. We need help. We're going to fix this."

"It's so huge, I don't know if we can," I murmur.

"We can," my mom says, in a voice so strong I almost believe her.

She leaves me standing alone in the center of the living room for a moment and then zips back into the room, keys in hand.

Before I have time to think about it anymore, my mom is pulling me toward the car.

"Let's go."

One good thing about living in a small town is that it's possible that, way back in high school, your mother was friends with the man who is now police captain. It means that he might listen to you when others might not.

"So you just remembered all this?" Captain Moeller asks, looking back and forth between me and my mom.

Captain Moeller may have a potbelly and a bald head, but he's got a kind face and, frankly, he's our only hope.

"Yes," I say sweetly. "I remember the day of the kidnapping now very clearly. I could help a sketch artist. Or look in a book?"

"They'd be a lot older now," the captain says softly.

He doesn't know what I see.

"We'd like to try," my mom says warmly. After exhaling loudly, Captain Moeller gets up. He grabs a binder from the shelf and tosses it on the small table in the corner.

Then he retrieves two more, each filled with photos, from the outer office.

"Start there, London," he says, then turns to my mom and offers her coffee. She agrees, and he leaves us alone.

"I don't think this is going to help," I whisper.

"Just try," my mom whispers back, bringing her chair over to join me at the table. She eyeballs the faces of criminals with me, even though she wouldn't know the culprits if they walked up to her at the bank.

The captain returns and does paperwork while my mom and I examine the photos of criminal after criminal. An hour later, my butt hurts from the hard chair, and I've got nothing except that creepy feeling you get from looking at people who might want to do you harm.

I want to go home and forget all of it. I want to watch a Disney movie to scrub my brain clean. But I know now that I can't. I've regained these horrible memories; all I can do is try to change the ones that are yet to come.

"How about doing a sketch?" I offer again.

"Like I said before, the couple you remember will be much older now. It probably won't do any good," Captain Moeller says.

"Couldn't you try that age-progression software on it?" I ask. I'll watch way too many crime dramas in my lifetime. "Do you have that here?"

The captain laughs a little.

"Smart kid you have there, Bridgette," he says to my mom.

"She sure is," Mom agrees.

Captain Moeller looks back at me. "Yes, we have that here," he says. "I'm just not sure it would work with a sketch. And besides, our sketch artist has gone home."

I glance at the industrial clock behind his head, as does my mom.

"Oh, Jim, I'm sorry to keep you," Mom says. "You need to get home to your family."

"It's okay, Bridgette," he says with compassion in his eyes. "Anything for you. I remember the incident like it was yesterday."

I break away mentally and force myself to remember anything that might help the situation. There is one thing: the piece of paper. The problem is that I remember it from the future.

My mom chitchats with the captain as I ponder ways to get him interested in the address. In the end, lying wins.

"Back when it happened, when they took Jonas, the woman dropped a piece of paper with a note on it in our car," I blurt out. Both adults snap to attention, Mom because she knows I'm lying and Captain Moeller because he seems to be the type of person who responds to carrots.

"What did it say?" the hound dog asks.

"Well, I'm not positive, but I think it was an address. There was something about Beacon Street. I remember because I thought it said 'bacon' at first." I blink twice like an innocent child. My mom's lips purse but she doesn't say anything. "I really like bacon," I add, feeling idiotic as soon as the words leave my lips. Thankfully, Captain Moeller ignores that part.

"No city?" he asks.

"No," I say, shrugging. Does he expect this to be handed to him on a silver platter?

"Well, I'll look into it," he says before his phone rings. He answers, talks briefly, and hangs up. My mom stands to leave. I follow suit. The captain walks us out and shakes both our hands. We leave, dejected and exhausted.

Halfway home, before we've finished ordering our drive-thru meals, Mom's cell rings. She answers, listens for a moment, and then pulls out of the restaurant sans food. We've turned around and are heading back toward the station before I have time to ask why.

"He said he'll explain when we get there," my mom says, sitting straight and gripping the wheel like it might fly off at any moment.

Captain Moeller is waiting for us at the front desk.

"Thanks for coming back," he says as the three of us rush to his office. I wonder what the hurry is.

Once we're settled, he explains.

"I did a quick search on Beacon, London, and it turns out it's a street in the city," Captain Moeller begins. "A squad there has been keeping an eye on a building on that street...suspicious activity, I guess. A friend down there was still at his desk: he told me that a man and wife recently rented the space—it's an office downtown in that older area—and anyway, there have been odd complaints, so they've been watching it."

"What type of complaints?" Mom asks, and I notice that she is clutching her purse like a life vest.

"Crying children late at night...in a business registered as a pawnshop," he says quietly. "The squad has done routine checks twice now and there's no sign of wrongdoing. But like I said, they're keeping an eye out."

Captain Moeller stops talking a moment and clears his throat.

I'm confused. My mom might be, too. I can't be sure.

"What does all this mean, Jim?" she says aloud. "Why did you want us to come back down here?"

"Well, that's the thing. It's touchy, and maybe I'm wrong, but this new information piqued my interest," the captain says, leaning back in his chair and running a hand through what hair he has left. He checks the clock and continues.

"You never did an autopsy on Jonas's body, did you, Bridgette?"

The question slugs my mom in the gut, and she looks visibly hurt for a split second. Then she recovers.

"No, you know that, Jim," she says. "There were his clothes—definitely his clothes—and with the decomposition, we decided it was enough."

My mouth is ajar now. Hasn't my mom seen a single crime drama? Maybe she just wanted it to be over. Maybe she just needed to believe, to bury him and move on.

"What does that have to do with anything?" Mom asks, seeming agitated now.

"I don't know. Kids late at night...at a pawnshop that the locals say isn't open in the daytime. It's just suspicious."

"Say what you mean, Jim," my mom barks, and suddenly Captain Moeller sits straight in his chair.

"It's possible that the pawnshop is a front for an illegal adoption agency. I think they might be stealing and selling kids."

My mom's jaw drops. "Selling kids?" she asks, clearly horror-stricken.

Captain Moeller rubs his eyes. "It happens more than you'd think. People can't have them on their own, and they get impatient because regular adoption takes too long. They turn to illegal baby brokers and fork out thousands to buy Junior, no questions asked."

My mom is quiet for a full two minutes before acknowledging the possibility. Finally, she dares to say it aloud: "You think they stole Jonas and sold him to new parents."

"It's possible," Captain Moeller replies. "I don't want to get your hopes up, but if that were the case..."

Mom grabs my hand before interrupting.

"Jonas could be alive."

43

My eyes are still closed, but I'm awake now. The air in the room has shifted.

"London?" my mom whispers. I ignore her. She whispers again, but not to me. The sound is softer, as if she's turned to someone in the hallway.

"I guess she overslept."

"Guess so," the voice whispers back. I wish everyone would shut up. It can't be time to get ready for school already.

"London, it's time to get up, honey. You're going to be late for school," my mom says in a singsong voice.

Finally, I let loose a long, audible groan and open my eyes.

My room is bright with the morning sun; apparently I forgot to shut the shades last night. The clock reads 7:00. Ugh. My mom stands in the doorway with a funny look on her face, blocking another person from view.

"What are you doing?" I ask, showing my displeasure.

"Good morning, London," she says awkwardly, ignoring my question. "Do you want to read your notes?"

I furrow my eyebrows at her, and she smiles like a pageant contestant.

"No," I grumble. "Who's with you?"

The mystery visitor shifts and the floor creaks. I sit up in bed and try to see around my mom. She stays where she is for a few seconds, then throws up her hands.

"Fine, I'll catch you up," she says, entering the room and sitting down on the desk chair. The visitor tentatively steps into the room, bearing coffee and a bag of something I hope is a scone. I admire his striking features, piercing eyes, flawlessly messy hair.

"Hey, Luke," I say, with undertones of seduction that I hope fly over my mother's head.

From my right, Mom gasps. Not the reaction I'd expected.

Luke looks surprised. Then thrilled. Then skeptical.

"You remember him?" my mom asks.

"Of course," I say, throwing her a look that says I think she's lost it.

"You do?" Luke asks. Now I'm furrowing my eyebrows at him, too. What is wrong with everyone?

"And you haven't looked at your notes yet today?" Mom asks incredulously. I wish she'd leave us alone, because I can think of a better way to spend the few minutes we have before school.

"Is that coffee for me?" I ask Luke, arms outstretched. Then I answer my mom: "No, not yet. Why? Why are you acting so weird?"

She lets loose a silly, girlish giggle, and Luke and I can't help but laugh with her. When we all compose ourselves, I ask, "What's funny?" which sends my mom into hysterics once again.

Luke crosses the room, hands me my coffee, and sits next to me on the bed. He kisses my cheek and says softly, "You remember me."

I think of Luke tomorrow; I remember him from next year.

"I get the feeling that I didn't before," I say, matching his low tone. Through her laughter, my mom excuses herself and leaves us alone.

"Nope," Luke says, eyes bright. "But you do now, and that's all that matters."

"Well, let me catch up," I say, grabbing the stack of notes off the bedside table. After I've reviewed them, my mood has changed.

"Luke, we need to talk."

"Is this about yesterday?" he asks, looking hurt.

"Yes," I say, thankful for the details. "It's pretty serious."

Luke tenses and shifts to face me. "You're not breaking up with me, are you?"

"No," I say with a little laugh, brushing his hair out of his eyes.

"Just go ahead," Luke says glumly.

I take a deep breath, and slowly, carefully, I tell Luke the story of the memory that I know, from my notes, came back to me yesterday. I still remember it today, so I don't need to look back at my notes to explain everything. I'm detailed but to the point, never wavering until the very end.

"And then I die?"

"Yes," I say, my eyes welling up with tears. Luke and I will have a great relationship. We'll talk about marriage, but he won't get the chance to propose. Instead, he'll die.

The color drains from Luke's face, but he doesn't cry with me. Instead, he's still, pensive.

"Are you all right?" I ask after I've dried my tears.

"I don't know," Luke says, still immobile. He holds his coffee cup awkwardly by his left leg. I take it from him and set it on the table.

"I'm sorry for telling you."

"No, don't be," he says. "I'd rather know."

I'm not sure I feel the same way about my own end, but I don't admit as much. Luke continues.

"I think knowing about it is better, because then maybe

I can avoid it. We can avoid it together," he says, with forced strength.

"I guess," I say, looking into his eyes.

"No, seriously. Okay, yes, this is pretty intense. I'm a little...I don't know. I can't quite process it all right now. But don't you think the advance warning gives me the advantage?"

"But, Luke, I——"

"No, really. You changed something with Page. You've changed other things, too. You can change this. It won't happen," he says with authority, as if he's trying to convince himself. I guess that's the best anyone can do with this information.

"Maybe you're right," I say calmly.

"I *am* right," he says, his voice increasing in volume. "You'll change your future. You'll save me."

"And what if I can't?"

"Then we just won't go down the alley. Trust me, it won't happen."

Luke hugs me tight and kisses me with such strength that I almost buy his story. But when he releases me, I see it flash across his eyes.

Fear.

Hoping to distract him, I offer my notes so that he can read up on yesterday's events while I get ready for school. As I shower, I can't help but wonder whether I did the right thing by telling him.

Then again, maybe he's right.

Maybe knowing how to avoid bad situations is enough.

Reaching for my fluffy white towel hanging on the hook, I think one thought over and over again: Please, be enough.

44

Jamie looks at me in Spanish class without grimacing, but the rest of the day is bleak. I float through school in a fog, asking myself questions I can't answer: Is my brother alive? Will Luke die the death I remember? Will I ever get to meet my father?

Surprisingly, the dad thing is heaviest today. I remember bits of him. I want more.

I want a dad.

I want *my* dad.

Before bed, I trudge in slipper-clad feet to my desk to power down my laptop. Just as I reach for the mouse, a message box pops up.

LJH6678: Hi. Are you awake?

I recognize Luke's screen name immediately; he'll have it for as long as I know him.

LondonLane: Yep, just getting ready to go to bed.

LJH6678: I won't bug you. Just wanted to say good night.

LondonLane: You're not bugging me!

I stand in front of my desk, staring at the screen, waiting. After a few seconds, he types back.

LJH6678: I'm glad you told me.

LondonLane: Are you? I'm still not so sure about it.

LJH6678: It was the right thing to do.

LondonLane: If you say so!

The tiny screen is blank for a bit. I check the clock and shift from one foot to the other before leaning over to type.

LondonLane: I should sleep....

LJH6678: Okay.

LJH6678: Wait London? I have a question.

LondonLane: Okay?

LJH6678: I've been thinking about all of this today, about you remembering our whole relationship.

I slide down into the chair so I can read easier and type faster.

LondonLane: And?

A little butterfly pokes me under the rib as I hit enter and wait for Luke's response.

LJH6678: And I've been wondering whether you remember everything.

I ponder the question for a moment, then type.

LondonLane: I'm sure I don't remember everything. I remember the future the way you remember the past. You remember the really good and bad and forget some of the middle, right?

LJH6678: Sure.

LondonLane: Same with me. Why?

LJH6678: Do you remember us having sex?

My hand flies to my mouth, and I look around my room for eavesdroppers, even though I know I'm alone. My stomach won't stop doing somersaults.

Luke learned that he's going to die young today and all he wants to ask me about is sex?

LJH6678: Well?

LondonLane: Truth?

LJH6678: YES!

LondonLane: Yes.

LJH6678: Not fair.

LondonLane: I know but listen. In the way that you probably choose not to think about things that you don't want to remember, I do the same. It helps things be a little bit...surprising.

LJH6678: Still not fair. When is it?

LondonLane: Not telling.

LJH6678: Seriously, not fair.

Checking the time again, I lean back in my chair and stretch. The day is wearing on me. I need sleep.

LondonLane: Luke, I have to go to bed.

LJH6678: I know, I know. Me, too.

LondonLane: See you tomorrow?

LJH6678: Want a ride?

LondonLane: Of course.

LJH6678: I'll bring you treats if you tell me the date.

LondonLane: You'll bring me treats anyway.

LJH6678: I'm going to have to work hard to surprise you, London Lane.

LondonLane: Yes, you are.

LJH6678: Night, beautiful girl.

LondonLane: Night, Luke.

45

It's the last day of my junior year but it might as well be the first. I know the layout of the school from next year, but everything else is gone.

There is no math class tomorrow to remind me where I sit today. There are no locker trips next week to tell me where mine is located now. Luke can't exactly escort me around like a guide dog.

"You'll be okay?" Luke asks as he grabs my hand. He looks almost as nervous as I feel. We're walking in from the student parking lot carrying matching half-empty lattes.

"I'll be okay. My mom wrote it all down for me."

"That was cool of her," he says. "Has she heard anything yet?"

"No, not yet," I say, feeling a heaviness in my chest that might not ever go away.

"At least I can get you to your first class safely," Luke says, pulling me up the main hallway. We stroll in easy silence, Luke angling me over a couple of times when I almost collide with other students. He laughs when he realizes that I'm looking at their shoes. He walks me to the door of my Pre-calculus classroom and kisses me good-bye.

"Good luck," he says.

"Thanks," I say back, wanting to handcuff myself to him and make him sit through all my classes with me. Instead, I force myself to go in.

After class, I hit my locker for a book to read in study hall. Luke reminded me to bring one, since Ms. Mason apparently gets mad when we talk to each other.

As I approach, I find Jamie standing there waiting for me.

"Hey," she says softly when I stop in front of the metal door.

"Hi," I say. We're both silent; I stare at my lock. Without tomorrow as reference, the combination isn't coming to mind. I pull out my cell, where it's stored.

"Thirty, twenty-two, five," Jamie says before I have the chance to look it up.

"You'll always have my back," I reply, spinning the dial.

"And you've always had mine," Jamie says.

I look into her eyes and know that this is it: we're okay.

"I'm sorry for getting so mad at you about…everything," Jamie begins.

"I'm sorry for the awful things I said," I reply.

"Do you remember what you said?" Jamie asks.

I cringe at that part in the notes. "Yes," I say. "I forced myself to remember."

"That was cool of you," Jamie says. She waits a beat and then gives me a quick hug.

"I missed you," she whispers into my hair.

"Same here."

"Liar," Jamie says playfully as she pulls away. "You can't even remember me. How can you miss me?"

"Oh, I remember you," I say. "Do you want to know all the things I remember?"

"No!" Jamie shouts with a laugh. "Keep your fortune-telling to yourself!"

Jamie and I link arms and start down the main hall. We laugh together as we walk, and I can't help but feel overwhelmed by Jamie's loyalty. Before we part, she turns to face me.

"Let's never fight again," she says.

"Agreed," I reply, knowing that really, other than small disagreements in college, we won't.

It makes me realize how much I appreciate Jamie's

willingness to trust me without knowing. She can't see what's coming. For Jamie, our relationship is a gamble. And yet she sticks with me. She keeps rolling the dice.

I stroll into the library for the last time this year, happy that my best friend is betting on us.

46

Hours later, after walking into the wrong classroom twice, seeing a little too much of Mike Norris (the boys' bathrooms near the History wing aren't properly labeled!), lunching with Luke, and handing in a year-end graphic design project that I could have purchased for $29.95 from CheatersRUs.com, for all I know, the school day and the school year are over.

Luke drives me home, holding my hand across the center console all the way. I feel like more than the year is ending, but I have my forward memories to prove that it's not. Still, there's something bittersweet about our kiss good-bye.

"Don't stay up too late tonight," he calls before I close the door.

"Yes, sir," I say, laughing and trying not to think of why he wants me to be well rested. I know, but I won't write it down tonight.

Some things should be a surprise.

Inside, I'm shocked to find my mother, home early, sitting alone at the kitchen table.

"How was your last day?" she asks, forcing small talk.

"Fine," I say. "I made it to all of my classes, eventually. I handed in that project. It went as well as possible, I guess. What's up, Mom?"

"They want us to come down to the station," she says nervously.

"They know something?" I can feel my brain pulling together pieces from memory and notes to form a complete picture.

"Yes." Mom stands, ready to leave.

We drive in silence the twelve minutes it takes from the garage to the parking lot in front of the police station. We wait two minutes to see Captain Moeller. When we're all settled in his office, he tells us that they have conclusive results.

I move to the edge of my seat. My mom covers her mouth with her hand, presumably to thwart an impending scream.

We wait.

Captain Moeller clears his throat.

I want to jump across the messy desk and rip the words from his voice box.

Finally, he speaks.

"The boy you buried isn't Jonas."

Captain Moeller's words hang in the air; I can almost see them floating there. No one speaks. No one moves. When I can't take the tension anymore, I ask the totally irrelevant question: "Who was it?"

"A Baby Doe, probably from another state. He wasn't in our missing children database."

Finally, sound comes from my mother's mouth in the form of a gasp.

"I know, it's terrible," Captain Moeller says to my mom.

"So what's next?" she asks through the fingers over her mouth.

"We reopen the search for Jonas," Captain Moeller says.

My mom looks a little like she's in shock. She doesn't reply, so the captain keeps going.

"I took the liberty of having the team use the aging software on the old photo we had of Jonas. We can put that image out over the wire and get people in the area on lookout."

"What if he's not in the area?" I ask.

"We'll distribute it nationally, too," he says to me.

"Can I see it?" I ask.

"Of course," he says. The captain rifles around on his desk for a bit and unearths a thick, worn file. I wonder how many times it's been opened over the past decade.

Captain Moeller pages through the file and pulls out an eight-by-ten photo.

"Here you go," he says, sliding it across the desk. My mom leans in to see but doesn't touch. Tears silently flow down her cheeks; she's so quiet I barely know she's there.

Captain Moeller hands her a tissue and leaves us alone. When he's gone, I pick up the photo for a closer look.

For some reason, a strange calm washes over me at the sight of him: my brother. My shoulders loosen and I exhale slowly.

It feels right.

He seems familiar.

"Do you remember him? From the future?" my mom asks in a voice so weak it's like she's a mouse.

Excited for a moment, I rack my brain for a memory of my brother—any memory other than the horrific one of him being taken.

"No, Mom, I don't," I say. It causes her tears to flow faster. Instead of comforting her, I continue to stare.

There's nothing there, and yet . . .

There's something.

Like that punch line of a joke you forget by the end, there's something.

And to me, right now, *something* is just fine.

47

Luke parks directly in front of a NO TRESPASSING sign on the barbed-wire fence that keeps us from driving off the incline. He kills the engine and the headlights along with it.

The town twinkles below, and I inhale the warm evening through the open windows.

"Did you bring me here to kill me?" I tease.

"Not tonight," he says warmly. "This is a do-over."

"Of what?"

"Of our first date," he says, staring into my eyes. "We fell asleep; you forgot to write it down. I've told you about it. You've probably read about the morning after..."

My cheeks flush.

"... but you didn't experience it. So I'm doing it again."

"You're awesome," I say, without thinking too much about it. Luke grins sheepishly and heads to the back of the van to get some pizza.

After dinner and a movie, Luke suggests stargazing and I wholeheartedly agree. He rolls up the windows, since the night air is growing chilly, and we lie together under the blanket Luke thought to bring, staring up through the moonroof to the universe above.

"We should talk about it," Luke says, face to the stars.

"About what?" I ask, but I think I know what he's referring to.

"About you suggesting we break up."

I scoot closer to him, if that's possible.

"It's not that I want to break up, I just said that it might be better. For you. It might change the future so that you don't get killed." I say the words without conviction.

"Being without you would never be better for me," Luke says, facing me. His tone is serious. "Do you understand that?"

"Yes," I say, because I do. Maybe I'm selfish, but I give in a little too easily. I don't really want to let him go. Maybe deep down I have more faith in my ability to change things than I'm willing to admit.

"Then let's forget all about it," Luke says as he grabs my hand.

"Agreed," I whisper, kissing him lightly on the cheek.

"So did you remember this night already?" he asks.

"Probably, but I guess I didn't want to spoil it," I say truthfully. "I didn't include it in my notes."

"And you remember the summer?" he asks.

"Yes," I say quietly.

"That's not fair," he teases.

"Poor baby!" I say. "But you have things that I don't. You remember when we met; I'll never know what that felt like."

Luke turns and kisses me gently and then a little more forcefully before we settle back to look at the stars. I snuggle close to the boy I don't ever want to lose, hoping that somehow I'll save him.

The memory of his death is still there, but so is hope. Right now, in Luke's arms, I feel confident and capable. I will save this boy. I will know the man.

Luke and I stay nestled together until he nudges me.

"We'd better get going," he says gently. I guess I dozed off. "I'm not letting you fall asleep without a note again."

"Why not?" I ask, stretching. I kiss him on the cheek and add, with a sly smile, "You don't have to worry, Luke. I'll remember you in the morning."

48

6/15 (Wed.)

Outfit:
   —Navy shorts and spotty tank
   —Red two-piece
   —White flip-flops (lost one at the lake)

IMPORTANT:
   Police found Jonas's kidnappers (they are
"cooperating," whatever that means). Mom already told
Dad. She's emotional but that's understandable. So am
I. I stared at an age-progressed picture of Jonas for

an hour, trying to remember him. Didn't work, but there's something there...not sure what it is.

    Other stuff:
    —Spent all day with Luke...floated on inner tubes at the lake. Made out a little in the water...and in the van...and in my room until Mom came home.
    —Jamie's in L.A. until next week
    —Call Dad

Nerves rage through me as I slowly, carefully dial.

This is our third phone call—the third of what I know will be many more. I woke up this morning remembering bits of him, but I know from notes those memories are new.

I hit the last number, and feel like I might throw up at the sound of the first tinny ring. Another sound, and I check the door to make sure it's shut. A third, and I wonder if he forgot.

Then he's there.

"Hello?" says a deep, gravelly voice that makes me both happy and sad at the same time. We're rebuilding our relationship, both in real time and in my memories, but I can't help but feel his underlying heartache.

"Hi, Dad. How are you?"

"I'm just fine, Pumpkin. What's new with you?"

He does that, I've noticed: diverts the conversation to me. He doesn't talk about himself; not yet, at least.

But he will.

I rub my fingers over the delicate beetle brooch that was my grandmother's. A note from last week said that it arrived in the mail shortly after our last phone call. Apparently he wanted me to have something of hers.

He could have just saved it and brought it with him when he visits at the end of the summer. It will be brief, but he'll come.

He doesn't know that yet, but I do.

"Not a lot is new on my end," I say breezily. "Just hanging out. Enjoying the summer."

"That's good," he says.

"Dad?"

"Yeah, Pumpkin?"

"Are you okay?"

"Of course I am," he says quickly, as if fathers can't be upset. "Why do you ask?"

"It's just that my note today said Mom called you... about Jonas's kidnappers." I feel funny talking about Mom; I know by the way Dad will look at her at my graduation that he still loves her deeply.

"Your note said that, huh?" Dad asks with a strange tone to his voice. My condition is still weird for him. He hasn't lived with it for all these years.

"Yes," I say quietly. "Anyway, I was just wondering how you're feeling about that."

"Well, I guess I'm feeling a mixture of things, London," he begins. "Probably like you and your mom are."

I'm silent, so he continues.

"Your mother said that the kidnappers are giving out names and addresses of the people who bought the babies, so that's encouraging."

"But they haven't heard anything about Jonas specifically?" I ask.

"No," Dad answers, adding, "your note didn't tell you that part?"

"No."

"I guess I'd say that the way I'm feeling is both heavy and hopeful," my dad says, which is exactly how I'd describe my own emotions right now. "I don't know, London. Most bad things in life take a while to sort out, but eventually they get sorted. Believing that there will be resolution to all of this has helped get me through some pretty rough years."

I'm not sure what to say; we're both quiet for a few moments. Then I switch it up.

"Tell me something about him," I say softly.

"About Jonas?" Dad asks, as if he doesn't know who I'm talking about.

"Yes," I say patiently. "Just something nice. Something I might not know."

"Hmm," Dad says as he pages through his functional memory. "He loved sweet potatoes?"

I laugh and Dad laughs and it feels almost normal for a moment.

"Okay . . ." I say through giggles. "What else?"

"He always chewed on your mother's cell phone. . . . No wait, I've got a good one! Jonas loved bouncy balls.

He'd waddle through the house, collecting any ball he could find, whether it was a real one or just something like an orange that looked like a ball. He'd say, 'ba, ba,' and point to whatever round object he wanted until someone gave it to him.

"At Christmas your mom decorated the tree a few weeks before the big day. It was when he was about a year and a half. He was so good; he didn't touch the ornaments, despite the fact that most of them were round.

"Finally comes Christmas morning, we're handing out gifts from under the tree, and I think Jonas thought, 'Oh, so this is the day we get to touch them!' He toddled on over and grabbed as many ornaments as he could, then proceeded to try to bounce them on the hardwood floor."

"They broke?" I ask.

"Of course," Dad says with a chuckle. "They were your mother's vintage ornaments. They shattered into little pieces all over the floor. Jonas loved the noise but was a bit more careful around bouncy balls after that.

"Anyway . . ." Dad says, his voice trailing off.

"Good story, Dad."

"Yeah," he replies, sounding nostalgic. "Maybe we'd better cut this short today. I've got some work to do outside and I don't want to keep you from that boyfriend of yours. What's his name again?"

"Luke," I say, knowing that he'll start remembering Luke's name soon.

"That's right," Dad replies. I have a feeling that the story about Jonas made him sad, and that he doesn't much feel like talking anymore. And that's okay.

I understand, because more than he could know, I understand him. It's all there, in this delightfully warped brain of mine. It's all there before he says it. It's all there before he does it.

I adore my father, and that adoration is based mostly on the relationship I know we'll have eventually. Because of that, cutting one call short doesn't bother me.

"Okay, Dad, we can pick this up next time," I say.

"Sounds good. Same day next week?"

The corners of my mouth turn up; we're on our way to better.

"Yes, Dad," I say. "Same day next week."

There is silence for a few seconds, and then:

"I love you, Pumpkin."

"I love you, too, Dad."

In the middle of the night, the memory rips me from a dead sleep. I switch on the lamp and wait for my eyes to adjust, then throw off the covers and run.

"Mom," I whisper loudly. She doesn't stir.

"Mom?" I say in a quiet speaking voice. Nothing.

I move closer and put my hands on her shoulders. I shake her lightly. When that doesn't work, I shake her harder and raise my voice. "Mom!"

She gasps, shoots upright, and blinks wildly.

"What's wrong?" she shouts. Her gaze moves from me to the door to the far wall to the window and back again.

"Sorry," I say, sitting down on the edge of her bed. "I didn't mean to scare you. Nothing's wrong."

She checks the digital clock on her nightstand. "Then why are you waking me up at two in the morning?" she asks.

I hold up the photo of Jonas.

"This isn't exactly what he looks like," I say as my eyes well up with tears.

She's confused for a blink, and then it's clear.

"How do you know?" she whispers, asking to be sure.

"I know because we'll meet him, Mom," I say, and as I do, I let myself remember him coming to our house at Christmas. I remember my parents joking about keeping the ornaments away from him, and his warm and wonderful laughter.

"He's all right?" my mom asks, in an even lower tone, as if she's afraid to speak it.

I nod my head. "Yes," I say.

"How do you know?" Mom asks again. I move toward her and wrap my arms around her. I speak into her shoulder as we hug.

"I know because I remember."

EPILOGUE

Written Sun., 7/10; add to notes every night.

Luke gave me a look tonight, one that made my insides twist. We were squeezed in with hundreds of other kids at the Weezer show (awesome, btw), and without saying a word or touching me or anything, Luke told me that he wanted us to be alone.

Suddenly, I got emotional thinking about how important the little moments with Luke are. Sure, I can remember many more from the future. But right now, it's new. Who knows, maybe that was the first time he's ever looked at me in exactly that way. And in less than two hours, it will be gone forever.

I was dwelling on that when I got home. I reread all my notes from high school so far, trying to soak up the stuff I forgot. But instead of reminiscing, I realized something major: I'm a lot stronger than I used to be.

Before this year, my past memory and parts of my forward memory were blocked, probably because of my brother's death—at least what we thought was his death—and Luke's future death. Not to mention my dad's part in everything. Then Luke's presence somehow helped me start to remember. He started a chain reaction that ultimately gave me back my brother and my father, which made my relationship with my mom better, too. In some ways you could say he gave me back myself.

I'm sure I've had some of these thoughts before, but as far as I can tell, I've never written them down quite like this. Even though it's late, I'm doing it now, because I have so much to be thankful for: a mother who loves me; a father who's in my life again; an amazing best friend; a brother I'll meet again soon.

And a gorgeous, supportive boyfriend who helped me realize that being normal is overrated.

This note is to remind me of all of my gifts, from the people in my life to the ability that I and I alone seem to have. Because, yes, maybe I'll always forget the past. But what I need to remember most is this:

I can also change the future.

ACKNOWLEDGMENTS

Don't forget to thank...

Resident comedian, chef, chief critic, and daddy extraordinaire: my husband. Loyal and loving, willing to read the same novel countless times, always with constructive things to say, you are my best friend in the world. Thank you. Thank you.

My gorgeous daughters. You have no idea how much you have inspired me. You are the reason this book happened; when I had you, anything became possible.

The clan. My mother, who said, "Of course you did" when I sold my first book; my father, who lovingly dubbed this story "weird" and suggested calling it *Scrambled Brains and Ham*; my sister, who is forever my cheerleader; my twin brother, eight years too late; and my middle brother, a writer, too. I am honored and blessed to have each of you (and your husband/wife/kids/dog) in my life.

Don't forget to thank...

Grandpa. You told me to hurry up and get the book published so you'd be alive to read it. I hope you're chuckling at these words from your easy chair right now.

The rest of my family, blood or otherwise, who have supported me through my life in countless ways. You know who you are. I love you all.

The *Forgotten* Book Club: Amy, Kristin, Judith, and Deborah, four genius women who raised their hands to suffer through early drafts of the novel. Your insights helped shape London's world. Thank you.

Friends who endured questions about everything from nursing home hours to high school class periods to digging up dead bodies. Especially Bill, who was my biggest high school connection.

Kings of Leon, for writing "Use Somebody," and my local radio station, for overplaying the crap out of it when I was working on *Forgotten*. It will always remind me of Luke and London.

Don't forget to thank...

The man who shocked me by writing back in seven minutes: Superagent Dan Lazar. You've expertly fielded more questions than a Magic Eight Ball, aren't ashamed to love *Project Runway* as much as I do, and might just never sleep. I wouldn't be here without you.

The rest of the Writers House gang: "Fave" Stephen Barr; foreign rights champions Cecilia de la Campa and Jennifer Kelaher; and my early advocates, Bethany Strout, Beth Miller, and Genevieve Gagne Hawes.

Don't forget...

My editors at Little, Brown, Nancy Conescu and Elizabeth Bewley. Thanks, Nancy, for fighting for me in the beginning and for keeping me on track. Thank you, Elizabeth, for holding my hand across the finish line. And thank you both for loving London and Luke almost as much as I do.

Ali Dougal and the rest of the gang at Egmont UK, and other editors around the world who have embraced *Forgotten*. Thank you for your support.

And, finally, my readers. Thank you for spending time in London's world. Thank you for taking the extra few minutes to read these acknowledgments. Thank you for making me want to write more books.

Thank you.

As a little girl, Daisy Appleby was killed in a school-bus crash. Moments after the accident, she was brought back to life.

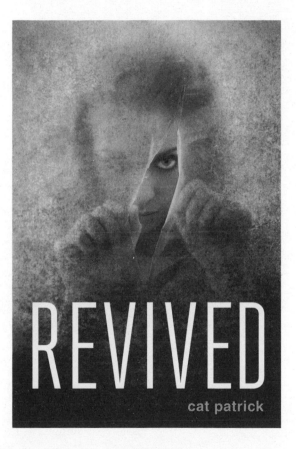

REVIVED

cat patrick

Turn the page for a sneak peek from Cat Patrick's riveting new novel, *Revived*, available in stores May 2012.

I'm flattened and thrashing on the sun-warmed track next to the football field, lying on what looks like asphalt but what I realize now that I'm down here is actually that fake spongy stuff. It reeks like it was just installed. There's a woman kneeling beside my right shoulder, shouting into a cell phone.

"Her name is Daisy...uh..." Sharply, she sucks in her breath. "I don't know her last name!" she cries.

For a split second, I don't know, either.

"Appleby," another teacher shouts.

"Appleby," the first repeats to the 911 dispatcher. "It looks like she's having an allergic reaction to something."

Bee, I try to say, but there's no air. No word.

My jerking limbs are like venomous snakes to the students forming a circle around me: The kids jump back in fear. I gasp with my entire body but only one rationed breath comes through. I know it's one of my last.

When my P.E. teacher told us to jog the outdoor track to warm up for volleyball, I was excited about the fresh air. Maybe I'd get a little color on my cheeks. But then a fuzzy yellow and black menace wanted to join me, and decided that maybe he'd invite a few friends, too. I hit number one on my speed dial the second I felt the familiar pinch of the first bee sting; I only hope Mason makes it in time.

A wave of calm begins to creep through my body: I know it won't be long now. Everything, forehead to toenails, relaxes. When the threat of getting kicked disappears, the crowd tightens around me. My eyes bounce off face after face hovering above me. They're all strangers; high school just started yesterday, and no one I know from junior high is in my P.E. class.

Most of them look terrified. A few girls are crying. The principal shows up and tries to contain the crowd, but they're like magnets, drawn in by the thrill of someone else's misfortune.

"Move back," he shouts. "Move back so the paramedics will be able to get through!" But no one listens. No one moves back. Instead, without knowing it, they form a blockade between me and help.

I lock eyes with a pretty, dark-skinned girl whose

locker is near mine. She seems friendly enough to be the last person I see. She's not crying, but the look on her face is pure distress. Maybe we would've been friends.

I stare at the girl and she stares at me until my eyelids fall.

The crowd gasps.

"Oh my god!"

"Do something!"

"Help her!" a guy's voice pleads.

I hear sirens approaching. Tennis shoe–clad feet thunder away from me, presumably to wave in the paramedics. I wonder whether it's Mason and Cassie or the real ones.

My arms go completely limp.

"Daisy, hold on!" shouts a girl. I like to think it was my almost friend, but I don't open my eyes to see for sure. Instead, my mind goes blank. None of the sounds are clear enough to hear anymore. The world fades to nothing, and before I have the chance to think another thought,

I'm dead.

"Do you have everything you need?" Mason whispers through the darkness as we walk briskly to the waiting SUV. It's the middle of the night in Frozen Hills, Michigan, and we're minutes from our next move.

"Yes," I say, confident that I've left nothing behind but furniture and off-season clothing. I've been through this before: I know the drill.

"Let me take that," Mason says, pointing to the suitcase I'm dragging behind me on the cobblestone walkway. I let him because I feel a little wonky from the procedure. Not quite myself yet. Mason grabs the bag and what was bricks to me is feathers to him: He tosses it on top of the other suitcases in the back and soundlessly shuts the vehicle doors.

I climb into the backseat. From the front, Cassie turns to acknowledge me momentarily before going back to her work. She's still sporting a fake paramedic outfit, but she's thrown a faded gray sweatshirt over the top. Her strawberry-blond hair is pulled back in a taut, efficient ponytail. She pushes her rimless glasses, which make her look older, up higher on her nose as she reads something from her government-issue supercomputer disguised as a smart phone.

I watch Mason head back inside for the final sweep, then admire the outside of the house I've gotten used to over the past three years. It's a two-story redbrick house with black shutters that was built when people still used the telegraph; it has its own creaks and character and I'm going to miss it. Moments from goodbye for good, I realize that this house was probably my favorite. Then again, maybe the next one will be even better.

I think about how I'll design my new bedroom until I see low headlights approaching. I get a charge when the black sedan pulls up and two men in dark outfits get out; it's always sort of thrilling to see the cleanup crew arrive. Though they've probably never been here before, they walk through the low black iron gate and up the porch steps without hesitation. Mason comes out just as one of the agents reaches for the front door handle. The men pass without speaking, giving one another nothing but quick chin dips.

I watch the door close behind the agents. Like an owl in the night, I search wide-eyed for movement inside the house, but the windows stay dark; the night stays still.

Unless you catch them going in, you can't tell they're there. Ninja stealth in black chinos and fleece jackets, they'll erase traces of me and my faux family and leave the house so authentically bare that the real estate agent who comes to sell it will never for a minute think it was inhabited by anyone other than a nice young couple and their ill-fated teen.

After they fix the house, the team will infiltrate the neighborhood long enough to put minds at rest, seeding gossip about the sad family returning to Arizona or Georgia or Maine to deal with the loss. The rumors are always started by the unrecognizable guy at the gas station or the mousy girl using the computer at the library.

The agents — the *Disciples* — are trained as doctors, scientists, watchers, and bodyguards, but I've always thought most of them could make it in Hollywood, too.

Mason, in his recurring role as Loving Father, finally climbs into the driver's seat. In worn jeans, loafers, and a cozy brown sweater, with his tired green eyes and messy dark (but prematurely graying) hair, he fits the role he's played for eleven years now.

"Where are we going?" Mason asks Cassie. Cassie doesn't look up from her tiny computer when she replies in her Southern-accented voice.

"Nebraska," she says. "Omaha."

Mason nods once and puts the SUV in reverse. I check my former home once more for signs that there are government agents inside: no luck. Then I exhale the day and the town away and stuff a pillow between my head and the cool window, and by the time we're down the driveway and turning off of our street, I'm asleep.

When I open my eyes, it's light outside. Bright light. The kind that makes me want to throw a rock at the sun. I have a crook in my neck and my mouth feels like I ate salty cotton balls. I look at Mason in the rearview mirror; he feels my stare and speaks.

"Hi there," he says. I can't tell whether he's looking at me or the road because he's wearing dark sunglasses.

"Hi," I grumble.

"How do you feel?" he asks.

"Headache," I answer.

"That's normal," he says.

"I know."

"Water," Cassie says, offering me a bottle without looking my way. I take it and gulp down half in two seconds, then look out the window to the unidentifiable landscape zooming by at seventy-five miles per hour.

"Where are we?" I ask.

"Illinois," Mason says.

"ILLINOIS?!"

Cassie jumps a little but still doesn't look back at me. I take a deep breath, which for some reason makes me yawn loudly. I rub the sleep from my eyes and in a more measured tone ask, "How long was I out?" Mason glances at Cassie and then checks the clock.

"I'd say you were probably out about eight hours," Mason says as plainly as if he's giving me a weather report.

"Eight hours? How is that possible?"

"They added a calming agent to it...to smooth the rough edges," Mason says.

I nod, still feeling woozy.

"Maybe they need to tone it down," I say. "Unless they're going for TKO."

"I'll make a note," Cassie says, her eyes still glued to her tiny phone screen. In private, Cassie is free to be her workaholic robot self.

"What's our new last name going to be?" I ask. With every new town comes a new last name; first names stay the same for the sake of consistency.

"West," Mason says.

"Huh," I answer, rolling it around in my brain. Daisy West. Definitely more interesting than Daisy Johnson from Palmdale, but maybe a little too cute. Though not nearly as bad as Daisy Diamond from Ridgeland.

"I think I liked Appleby best," I conclude aloud.

"You were more used to it," Mason replies. "West is fine."

Shrugging, I consider my options for passing the time.

"I wish we could fly," I murmur to myself, but Mason hears me.

"That would be nice," he agrees. Unfortunately, our fourth passenger, Revive—the top secret drug that brings people back from the dead—makes that impossible. The drug is too precious to check and too secret to carry on. So every time we move, we have to drive; every time we drive, I'm at a loss about what to do. I wish I could read, but it makes me carsick, and since we left so suddenly, my iPod isn't charged. Eventually I settle on counting mile markers until I think I might pee my pants. I ask Mason to pull over at a diner, then, considering it's almost noon and all, we decide to eat, too.

After visiting the surprisingly inoffensive bathroom, I join Mason and Cassie at a booth in the back. They're sitting across from each other but aren't speaking; they look like a typical married couple. I make a split-second decision and scoot in next to Cassie, opting to pretend to be a mama's girl. Cassie looks up at me and smiles warmly.

We're in public now, so she's human.

"You're the spitting image of your mom," the waitress says to me when she comes to take our order. We've heard it before, but it's a false comparison. Cassie's brand of blond is straight with reddish tones, while mine is wavy and so dirty it's essentially light brown. Cassie's eyes are round and dark blue like the ocean, whereas mine are lighter than the sky at noon, wide set and almond shaped. She's nearly six feet tall, and I'm five foot six; she's curvy, and I can wear jeans from the boys' department.

But what makes the "look-alike" comment even more absurd is the fact that Cassie's only thirteen years older than me.

And yet, we play the part.

"Thank you!" Cassie says, hand to chest like she's beyond flattered.

"Uh, yeah, thanks," I mutter, hoping that I'm coming off as a typical teen who doesn't care to look like her mother. In truth, despite the fact that she barely has a personality, Cassie's pretty. I'm fine with people saying I look like her.

"You're most welcome," HELLO, MY NAME IS BESS replies. "Now, what can I bring you?"

I order a veggie burger and a chocolate shake; Mason orders coffee and a Spanish omelet; and Cassie orders a hard-boiled egg, dry wheat toast, and sliced melon on the side.

Bess writes in her notepad and leaves. Then, almost too soon for it to be made to order, the food rides in on Bess's wide arms. Quickly, she sets down plates, fills coffee cups, and pulls ketchup out of her apron pocket.

"Need anything else?" she asks. Three head shakes and she's gone.

We eat in silence, me downing my lunch as if I've never tasted food before, then wondering if the scientists at the big lab added a metabolism booster to Revive in addition to the calming agent. Knowing it's silly, I don't ask Mason about it. But I can't help but notice that Mason's and Cassie's plates are still half full when mine is all but licked clean.

"So, why Omaha?" I ask as Mason takes a bite of his

omelet. I watch his jaw muscles flex as he chews slowly, deliberately. After he swallows, he speaks.

"It's one of his favorite cities," he says.

Mason means the Revive project mastermind. Basically invisible and in control of a program that brings people back from the dead, he's earned the nickname God.

"Why?" I ask.

"Because it's moderate, I suppose. Not too small or too big. Rarely in the news. Friendly. Reasonably gentrified. You know what that means, right?"

I roll my eyes at him.

"So, all in all, it should be a good cover. Assuming..."

"Assuming what?" I ask.

Mason checks the tables around us, then answers in a low tone. "Assuming nothing *else* happens."

"I didn't mean to do it, you know," I say quietly.

"You never do," Mason says, holding my gaze. "But you didn't have your EpiPen, either."

"I forgot it," I say quickly.

It's a lie.

In truth, I spent way too long deciding what to wear, leaving only five minutes to arrange my hair into something resembling a style. I left for school in a rush, remembering the EpiPen, which probably would have saved my life, halfway down the block. I wasn't so late that I couldn't have gone back, but for some reason I didn't.

Having been trained to know when people are lying, Mason narrows his eyes at me. I assume Cassie's doing the same, but I don't look at her to find out. For a moment, I think Mason's going to call me on it, but thankfully, he moves on.

"Daisy, I think you should know that we nearly couldn't bring you back this time," he says so quietly it's almost like he's breathing the words. His bluntness, I'm used to—Mason treats me like a partner, not a daughter—but I'm surprised by the idea of permanent death.

"Was it a bad vial?" I ask.

"No, it was fine," Mason says. "It was . . . you."

"He almost called time of death," Cassie interjects. Stunned, I look at her, then back at Mason.

"Seriously?" I ask.

"It was very stressful," Mason says. There's a flicker of something like worry in his green eyes, and then it's gone.

I think for a moment before coming to what I consider to be a pretty rational conclusion: "But it did work, so everything's fine."

"But it might not be next time," he says. "I'm merely advising you to take precautions. Don't you remember Chase?"

My stomach sinks as an old memory sets in: Seven years after the bus crash that started it all, Chase Rogers died again, for seemingly no reason. He was Revived repeatedly, but—Mason told me—he seemed to have developed an immunity to the drug. Then he died for good.

"I'm not like him," I say quietly. Bess comes and sets down the check, which silences us for a few minutes.

"I'm not like him," I say again when the coast is clear.

Mason looks deep into my eyes. "I hope not. Just be more careful, all right?"

"All right," I agree.

Another family is seated at the booth directly behind us, so the conversation is over for now, at least.

"Are my gorgeous ladies finished eating?" Mason asks loudly enough for others to hear. The mom at the table behind us sighs. Mason can be charming when he wants to.

I look down at my plate, which has discarded raw onions, wilted lettuce, and a quarter of a pickle left on it.

"Uh...yeah," I say in my best disinterested-teenager voice.

"I sure am," Cassie says, patting her flat stomach. "I'm stuffed to the gills."

"Great," Mason says. "Then let's clear out."

We walk up to the front counter. As we wait for Mason to pay, Cassie fixes a stray piece of my long hair in that absentmindedly automatic mom-ish way. She looks at me with love; I roll my eyes and brush her hand away.

After Mason leaves a five on the table for Bess, he opens the OUT door, causing the bells on top to jingle, and holds it for his wife and daughter. In the parking lot, when we're still visible to the other diners, I stare at the ground and walk three steps behind my parents while they hold hands and Cassie laughs at nothing.

Then we get in the SUV and drive away.